Wonderboy

Tom Conyers, an award-winning filmmaker (The Caretaker – 2012), is also a poet, playwright, painter, illustrator and photographer. To check out his other work, including novels *One Shot, Forever Human* and *Morse Code for Cats,* and his poetry and drawing collection, *The Crime of Rhyme*, please visit his website:

www.tomconyers.com

ARRANT
PRESS

For Mum & Dad

WONDERBOY

life is only what you wonder

TOM CONYERS

WONDERBOY

Copyright © Tom Conyers 2014
www.tomconyers.com
Published by Arrant Press
P.O. Box 406, Burwood VIC, Australia 3125

ISBN-13: 978-0980587142 (Arrant Press)
ISBN-10: 098058714X
**Edited by Bryony Sutherland
Cover Design, Typesetting &
Photography by Tom Conyers
Models: Charlie & Maddie**

Chapter 1

The Adelaide Hills, Australia, 1975

Jack Bennett was running late. His mother, Jean, had already called three times to say his older brother Simon was ready to leave for school. Jack looked round his room once more – there was always some schoolbook he was reprimanded for forgetting to pack. Jean called a final time, judging from her tone. He hoisted his old-fashioned, leather bag over his shoulder; all his classmates had vinyl.

'Your toast,' she said, when he emerged from his room. Jean was tall and willowy, with a beautiful aquiline nose and slightly wavy ebony hair. Everyone said Simon took after her. She was wearing one of the red cardies she'd knitted herself.

Jack generously spread his toast with Vegemite and hurried outside, getting doused with sunlight; it would be a hot day. He hated hot days, which seemed to be the norm where they lived. Everyone else wore shorts in such weather but he felt silly exposing his knees. He looked at his covered legs. Was it too late to change his woollen trousers for the norm? Jean's expression as she appeared at the front door decided him to keep moving.

Shoving his toast in his mouth, he grabbed his green, rickety bike from under the iron veranda. He could see Simon was already a long way up their dolomite drive, about to disappear at the point where the road was arched by three River Red gums with impressively long reaches.

His father, Daniel, was filling his Holden station wagon with the paint tins he needed for work. Daniel also had dark hair that made Jack's blondeness even more surprising. (Although Jean told Jack his was the sort of blonde that would be brown by the time he was twenty.) Daniel was wearing his paint-smattered overalls. His eyes were blue like Jack's, but a washed-out version.

'See you, son.'

Jack took the half-eaten toast, with its Moorish arch, out of his mouth.

'Bye, Dad.'

Daniel tousled Jack's hair and watched as his son pedalled in pursuit of Simon.

Passing under the tunnel of gum leaves, Jack emerged into the glare again, spying Simon nearly at the top of the hill. He was still riding sitting down, whereas Jack had to stand for strength to get up the steep slope.

Simon, at fourteen, wasn't thin and gangly like Jack, but already filled-out for a kid. The muscles he was building playing football would soon iron out any familial lankiness even more.

The road levelled out and Jack could sit down to ride like his brother. But still he'd never catch up to him! A friendly toot came from behind; his father in his tan station wagon. Daniel leant out the window.

'Catch a ride.'

Still pedalling, Jack held onto the open back window. He smiled as they passed Simon, who yelled out, 'Cheat!' Arriving at the pipe gate with its diagonal bar going down to the bottom hinge, Jack let go and careened to a halt. He threw his bike down on the long grass. Slipping the wire off the iron knob on the striated post, he opened the gate for his father. Uncharacteristically, Daniel neither thanked him nor waved goodbye as he drove through; his eyes were focused elsewhere.

Jack also looked across at the next-door neighbour's fence. To his surprise, two labourers (Kim Mitchell's sons, friends of Jean) were removing the boards barring the gate. As far back as Jack could remember, the next-door neighbour's property on that side had been vacant, house *and* land.

Daniel drove off slowly on the bitumen road, still focused on the property. Jack turned back to the two lads who were levering off the last board.

It was odd all right, after all these years, that the place should be unsealed now. In all his eleven years, Jack had never known it to be tenanted.

Daniel let his sheep roam there now and then to keep down the grass and minimise the threat of fire. Once Jack had asked him why the owners (wherever they were) didn't sell. He'd answered in an odd, dreamy way: 'Perhaps she can't bear to.' Just who 'she' was, Daniel didn't say.

Jean forbade Jack and Simon from hopping over the fence, except for when they were helping Daniel round up sheep.

The brothers used to muck about there, regardless. The large old house had been boarded up as well, but they could explore a series of ruined settlements dating from Australia's colonial past situated to the back of the property. There were gnarled orchards and an amazing overgrown garden hidden inside one of the roofless stone buildings. In this garden, they were doubly forbidden to play, again on Jean's command. The reason given:

the crumbling walls of the settlers' huts were old and could collapse any moment.

They looked sturdy enough to Jack.

He loved the sequestered secretiveness of the place. Unfortunately, in recent years, Simon had lost what little interest he'd ever had in it. Now Jack, if he trespassed at all, was obliged to do so alone. He never tarried, though. Before long, some sound, some shadow, either in the orchard, under the veranda, or by the horse stalls, would spook him and he'd run back home. The secret garden compelled and frightened him most. It was shadowy, yes, but the most worrisome part was its deep … *sadness*. Did people get to feel this sad?

'Beat you!'

Jack could kick himself. All that daydreaming meant Simon had ridden past him on his super-slick red bike and sped through the open gate.

'Hey, wait!' yelled Jack.

He pushed his bike through, hurriedly threw it against the other side of the wood post, and shut the gate, looping the iron noose over the bent railway bolt. He ran alongside his bike before stepping up on the pedal and throwing his other leg over. But still he hadn't been quick enough; Simon had already forged a strong lead.

As Jack's legs pistoned, his mind wandered again.

If only Simon still liked to play make-believe, just as he had before the encroaching teenage years stole his thoughts elsewhere. Sometimes Daniel would play with Jack after work, but he was often tired and Jean would have chores lined up for him.

The two cycled along, the distance ever growing between them. The road stretched over the hills like a sunning snake. Great, rolling brown hills fell away either side. Trees huddled in clumps, sheep in aggregates, and cows were spread out, munching, while telegraph wires casually bisected the land in sagging lines, their wires argent in the morning sun.

A *brrrm* of an engine and Jack glanced to his right to see a red-and-white striped Cessna plane flying low over a furrowed field belonging to the Harrows. It banked sharply to the left, releasing its spray. Immediately, Jack's mind improved on the situation. To him, the sky was now dark with clouds. The Cessna swung round ahead of them and disappeared into the storm's thick, black centre.

He yelled to Simon, 'Hey, stop!'

The plane re-emerged. But no longer was it a Cessna: in Jack's eyes, it was now a World War II spitfire, khaki green, with mad red eyes painted under its wings.

Simon braked and stood astride his bike, craning his neck to stare at Jack. The Spitfire dropped out of the sky and soared down the road at them.

'Oh, no,' thought Jack, as the plane opened fire with its twin machine guns, the sides of the road popping up with dirt either side of Simon.

Jack yelled a warning but Simon merely stared, refusing to understand. Jack dived into the side ditch, which was suddenly a trench in a combat zone, ringed with barbwire. Jack, armed with a Sten gun, fired at the belly of the spitfire as it flew overhead.

With its passing, the sky cleared. Simon was looking down at Jack, his square shoulders framed in cerulean blue. Sheepishly,

Jack put down the stick he was holding. Simon merely shook his head.

As Jack dusted himself off and righted his bike, that overgrown garden flashed across his mind. For the first time, it worried him that no one tended it. He wondered for whom the labourers were removing the boards.

And just who was this 'she' his father had mentioned so dreamily?

Jack didn't even try to keep up with Simon for the rest of the ride to school and nor did Simon slow his pace.

Chaining his bike next to Simon's at the school gate, Jack headed into the grounds, where he could see a futuristic-looking beetle-green Citroën DS parked outside Mr Higgins' office. Higgins was the headmaster, and generally considered benign by the other kids, but Jack avoided him where possible all the same.

Just then, Higgins walked out of his office in his perennially grey gabardine trousers and overcoat. Beside him, was a lady in a long flowing maxi dress, pulled in at the waist with a yellow belt. She wore an antique, floppy hat adorned with fresh gardenia, but this could not hide her abundant blonde hair, streaked with fawn. Her face was beautiful, her expression, kind. At her side was a tomboyish-looking girl, about Jack's age, in a collared green shirt, rather brave flared trousers and brown boots.

Higgins awkwardly opened the driver's door for the lady, while the girl hopped in the passenger side.

Higgins had the largest forehead Jack had ever seen. It somehow contrived to give him a constantly startled appearance and today was no different. He noticed Jack, meaningfully tapped his similarly oversized watch, and nodded towards class.

As Jack trundled off, he had the unreal sense that he'd never before seen such an elegantly attired and poised creature to grace Miller's Creek. That lady seemed better suited to TV or even the movies.

Miss Jackson was about the same age as Higgins: mid-fifties. But to Jack, she was simply an adult of the more archaic variety. She had jet-black hair, impossibly straight, that sat atop her head like a lacquered helmet, enlivened by the odd strand of grey. Her nose was beaklike and she always wore dark skivvies, tartan grey dresses, black stockings and black shoes with brass buckles – everyone wondered where she bought them, they were so out of style! She had a funny way of standing, as though her elbows were attached to her body, forcing her to lean back to see and co-ordinate whatever her hands were doing.

At that moment, she was awkwardly copying notes from her red book onto the blackboard, which meant a lot of bird-like peeping up and down.

'… and then came the Jurassic Period, and that's when the biggest reptiles roamed the earth. What we call the dinosaurs.'

Jack surveyed his class, heads tilting from the blackboard to their books, studiously copying. The two- seat wooden desks (still with their inkwells despite the Bic pen having been introduced to schools ten years previously) were divided in two columns, with room to walk down the middle. Miss Jackson insisted the girls sat on one side, the boys on the other. Jack was thankful Miss Jackson made the girls sit in the windowless part that joined the corridor wall, to 'look after their skin', because he liked to stare through the glass.

There was nothing outside the window except, parallel to theirs, another portable classroom jacked-up on Besser bricks, containing another odd teacher and another bored bunch of students copying boring notes.

'... and after the Jurassic Period, came the Cretaceous ...' droned Miss Jackson.

Jack loved dinosaurs. His father had bought him many a Methuen book on those ancient reptiles (or had people decided they were birds now?) but somehow Miss Jackson had the knack of making even exciting things dull.

Michael snorted in the seat next to him. Michael had curly brown hair and his nose was always grotty, like he was still in prep. It left him with a perpetual hint of a Hitler moustache. He and Jack had next to nothing in common, except they each had no one else with whom to share a desk.

The bell rang. Jack turned from the window to Miss Jackson. She frowned before carefully marking her spot in her red book with its bound green ribbon. She scrutinised the class and frowned again.

'All right, off to lunch.'

The students began to move in a single great clattering commotion. Miss Jackson's face tensed like she'd been electrocuted.

'Class!'

Obediently, they resumed their seats. Miss Jackson allowed herself a tight smile.

'Girls first.'

The girls got up quietly and filed out, some of them beaming at the boys. Jack stared out the window again, wondering if this was how things were meant to be. He heard Miss Jackson signal that the boys could leave next. As they got up noisily around him, Jack wondered if he'd be less alone in that garden. Could he and it be alone *together* somehow?

When the noise had moved to the corridor, he stood, only to lock eyes with Miss Jackson. She had a flat silver flask to her lips, which she quickly lowered. Somehow he knew that, like him, she had thought the class empty. With a bitter grin, she tightened the lid on the flask and put it in the drawer, which she then locked with an iron key.

The smell as Jack passed was strong and sweet and acrid.

His lunch was what his mum always made him. Contained in a plastic red lunchbox, that had three jutting partitions, it held a frozen orange juice container (usually melted by lunchtime); a sandwich kept fresh in Glad Wrap (lettuce and Vegemite); and fruit of some description (usually an apple or orange. He'd eaten today's apple at recess).

He was sitting on a large tractor tyre, which made up one component of the school play equipment. On the brown, dusty oval, Simon was standing with several kids his own age, among them the ever-popular Troy. They were engaged in an unsuccessful game of cricket with a mismatching half-set of bats, stumps and ball. For the first time consciously, Jack worried that he wanted to be alone. No, not alone. But if this was company, then he knew he preferred his own. And then he knew, just as spontaneously, just as intuitively, that he shouldn't.

'Who wants to play Red Rover?' yelled Simon.

'Me!' shouted the kids around him.

Jack jumped off the tyre, hoping the movement would signal engagement.

Fatty stepped forward. '*I* wanna be captain.'

The older kids laughed.

'Not you, Fatty,' said Simon. 'Adrian is.'

Adrian, a fourteen-year-old with a cowlick and a scar on his chin from a car accident he couldn't stop boasting about, dropped the plastic bat and stepped in front of Fatty.

Fatty looked defeated already yet spoke up. 'But who's the other captain?'

Troy ogled Fatty like he was stupid. 'Me and Simon, of course. Line up, the rest of you.'

The kids spread out in a half-circle in front of the self-appointed three. Simon directed the first finger.

'Sean.'

A buoyant, stocky kid jogged the three steps into their ranks.

'Thanks, Simon.'

Adrian was quick to choose next, not wanting to be deprived of the best players remaining.

'Bill, over here.'

As Troy mostly chose his and Simon's side, Jack saw his chance. He stepped beside his brother and pulled Simon's pale blue shirtsleeve.

'Simon, can you pick me?'

Simon shoved him away without turning. 'Bugger off.'

Jack steadied himself and tried again. 'Please, Simon, I won't annoy you.'

Simon scowled. 'Piss off.'

'I'll tell Mum,' said Jack, then immediately regretted that tactic.

'She won't care.'

Jack stood back and knew deep in his mind that his failure was broader than merely this one game. He had found himself watching again. Watching, like he watched his favourite TV show, *Doctor Who*. Only, that was a life of wonderment, not wondering, a world he felt more upset to be excluded from, than this mere colourless one before him.

Of the children still to be chosen, only Jack, and the other kids his age, Michael, Noel and Fatty, were left. Troy turned to Simon with a flick of his fringe, indicating with a broad grin that they were a poor lot. Simon shrugged, unconcerned; it was Adrian's pick anyway.

'All right: Noel.'

'Yippee!'

Michael and Fatty shifted dejectedly. Troy regarded them uncharitably.

'Pick me, Troy!' cried Michael.

Troy spat, like he'd seen his favourite cricketers do on TV. 'You can't tackle, Michael.'

'No, Troy,' piped up Fatty. 'Pick me!'

Troy leant forward to give his fringe a twirl before throwing his head back and catching it behind his right ear. 'You can't even run, Fatty. Who do ya reckon, Simon?'

Simon stared guiltily off to the side. Jack looked down at his feet. A moment later, he gazed up again at his brother, expecting Simon's eyes to be elsewhere. But they were locked on his.

'Jack,' Simon muttered.

Troy shot Simon a glance, unable to believe his friend's weakness. Simon stared back apologetically.

Jack stepped forward, smiling within. His second chance.

Chapter 2

'Oomph!'

His face hit the dirt. Adrian was on his back, gripping him in a bear hug. All Jack could think about at first was how baked the grass smelt, with its bits of rubbish and ants crawling through it. But then he thought about his staggering failure: it was his team's turn to run the gauntlet, and he'd been brought down first.

Adrian let more of his weight down on him, and stuck his chin near his, showing off the scar from his famous car crash. Jack spluttered for air. Eventually Adrian climbed off and Jack, wheezing, rolled on his back.

Troy was peering down at him. 'You're out.'

Jack sat up painfully but did not budge.

'You're *out*,' Troy repeated more loudly, tapping Jack on the shoulder to get his attention.

On his feet now, Jack tried to catch Simon's eye. Simon found sudden interest in a grass stain on his elbow. Jack walked back to the tractor tyres, half wishing he could roll away in one of them.

Miss Jackson poured a bag of sand into a large, capacious, metal tray that was sitting on her desk. She had everyone's attention, even Jack's. This looked promisingly arty to him, and art was what he was good at.

She spread out the sand with her long fingers.

'To continue with our theme of dinosaurs, we are going to make a diorama.'

The class strained forward, wondering if they could leave their seats and gather round the tray.

Miss Jackson brushed the grains from her hands.

'The boys can empty the other bag of sand ...' she said, looking up with a squint '... because that's the dirty job, while the girls can make the palm trees.'

She clapped her hands with a sharp, dry sound, and they got up.

Jack was disappointed he couldn't help make the palm trees. He watched enviously as the girls taped rolled-up cylinders of green-coloured paper together, then, at one end, cut lengthways, folding the resultant strips back to replicate palm fronds. But it was a technique Jack could show his father. He could also see a way to improve it. Instead of just the one sheet of green paper, why not roll up two (even three!), but each of a different hue to make tri-coloured palms? It was an idea, all right – one he could save for home.

The boys, apart from emptying then sculpting the last of the sand, were also given the task of positioning rocks and gnarled pieces of wood among the miniature dunes. These, too, could have been better chosen, and he wished Miss Jackson had let them know what was planned before dismissing them for lunch. He would have much preferred to search the school grounds for treasures than attempt to play Red Rover.

Theatrically, Miss Jackson, as if landing a rocket on the moon, placed the last palm tree in the sand.

'There! Now for the inhabitants.'

She unlocked the drawer to her desk and reached in. Jack thought of the rectangular silver flask. Instead, she withdrew a small, plastic bag filled with green-black shapes. She emptied these onto her palm, revealing them as rubber dinosaurs, each the size of a fifty-cent coin. Jack screwed up his nose. With the palms being pencil-height or taller, she had the scale all wrong. Oh well, he and Dad would do something similar at home, only much better executed. As Miss Jackson placed the dinosaurs in different positions, she counted slowly.

'One ... two ... three ... four ... five. Five! Remember that. There are five toy dinosaurs. So, if any go missing, and I'm not directing this at the girls, I'll get you. I mean it.'

Glancing round the circle, she seemed to peck each boy with her beaky nose. All the boys, and many of the girls, peered back timidly over the sides of the sand-tray. Miss Jackson, seemingly satisfied judging by her smile, stepped towards the wide sill of the window nearest her desk. Upon it stood a plastic pot of Geraniums, flowering white. She often called this profusion 'Miss Prunella', and had told the class they needed to whisper sweet nothings to plants to help them grow. Drawing her mumbling lips from the petals, and with her back still turned to her students, she abruptly uttered, 'Play!'

At once the faster children made for the dinosaurs, and those who managed to grab them first began to invent games for themselves. Michael, who had nabbed the tyrannosaurus, nudged Jack as if to say, 'Watch this' before making it mount the diplodocus that another student, Kate, had commandeered.

'Urgh! Michael!' spluttered Kate, her two looped ponytails making her look like a double-handled teacup.

Jack laughed. Kate let go of her dinosaur, and rushed to Miss Jackson. Jack stopped laughing when he saw the two return and stand behind him and Michael. Miss Jackson thrust her watering can into Kate's arms (the water dousing the tea cup's grin). Jack was about to alert Michael when Miss Jackson grabbed Michael by the neck. She pushed him up against the table, the miniature desert quaking and several palms toppling over.

'Michael, you filthy boy! How dare you? How dare you!'

Higgins was in the adjacent school corridor, sticking a poster on the cork notice board to do with rules for the students about not running, eating, or raising voices inside. To his surprise, he could hear what sounded like a teacher shouting. That shrill voice could only belong to Miss Jackson. He shook his head: he thought she had got past that nonsense.

Michael's nose was dripping as Miss Jackson pushed his dirty brown top up round his neck.

'That's how it starts,' she snapped. 'It just takes one filthy boy ...'

Higgins, trying not to run and break his own rules (it seemed he was going to have to be an example to student and teacher alike) trotted along the corridor to her classroom.

He could now hear the pleading tones of what sounded like Michael's voice, by comparison a soft accompaniment to Miss Jackson's percussion.

'I wasn't doing anything! Please, Miss Jackson!'

Jack didn't know what to do, if there was even anything as a kid he *could* do. The tray was looking precariously like falling off the desk – Miss Jackson had Michael shoved up against it so hard. Before it could topple, she yanked him away and smacked him across the face, sending him flying to the floor. Scrabbling to a sitting position, Michael looked up at her in horror. Jack decided to fetch Higgins. Ducking away, he noticed Higgins' face framed by the glass in the door.

'I wasn't doing anything, Miss Jackson!' squealed Michael. 'Please!

Jack was the only one to notice the door open. Miss Jackson grabbed her metal ruler off the dusty sill below the blackboard, and raised it above Michael.

'Liar!' she screamed. 'I *saw* you!'

She took a step towards him.

Higgins shut the door. Miss Jackson swung round, ruler still raised. The scared faces of thirty kids scanned between the two adults. The end-of-school bell sounded, and the class swayed towards the one exit, but with feet still timidly planted.

Miss Jackson lowered the ruler but kept her chin held high. Higgins looked from the class to Miss Jackson then back at the kids again.

'All right, class dismissed.'

This time, Jack didn't dally. He grabbed his books and pencil case and was out of there every bit as fast as his fellow students. Michael wouldn't look at Jack as they escaped the school grounds. But Jack could see his friend's nose was running profusely now, and his eyes had started leaking, too.

The sky was darkening with afternoon leading to evening, the brilliant blue muddying to a reddish brown. Jack was amid the clump of appropriately named ghost gums that edged his property and hugged the neighbour's. He was playing with a stick and pretending to be a Dalek from *Doctor Who*.

He wished his father could have played with him, but Jean had made sure he was busy fixing one thing or another for her. Simon had wanted to go for a jog, and nothing could persuade him otherwise. Thus Jack in his present state: left to make-believe on his own.

He didn't even have a pet.

Daniel used to have two dogs: lithe kelpie-crosses. One day, when Jack was about six, they came home with bloodied throats. John Harrow, Emma's dad and the owner of the property on the other side, reckoned they had mauled six of his sheep. Daniel compensated him but John still threatened to shoot the dogs. Now they'd got the taste, he reckoned they wouldn't stop. Daniel asked to borrow John's gun, then took the dogs one at a time behind the settler's huts. Those two shots felt like they echoed throughout the day.

Jack shook himself free of the memory and swung his stick around. He modulated his voice to sound high-pitched, mechanical.

'Exterminate! Exterminate! Resistance is useless. Resistance is ...'

He could see movement at the front of the neighbour's house, under the stepped gable. He dropped the stick and edged forward to the wire fence, making sure to keep low in the scrub. Upon the wires hung pendants of wool, where sheep had rubbed to alleviate their itches. The oily rich smell was pleasant to his nose.

The same truck he'd seen at the front gate in the morning, now pulled up at the front door. Kim Mitchell's sons jumped out of the cabin. For the first time ever, Jack saw a light go on in the house and then, even more remarkably, a lady dressed in a long, sheer gown appeared from under the sagging front veranda. The Mitchells wolf whistled. Although in shadow, he was sure it was the same woman he'd seen leaving Higgins' office that day at school. He wondered where the girl might be.

To get closer, Jack climbed through the fence wires and scrambled over the moist bracken. This was more fun. It involved other people … sort of.

The Mitchells pulled the bolts from the truck's back door, which then dropped with a thunderous bang.

In Jack's head, the unmistakable electronic opening bars from the *Doctor Who* theme music began to rumble. At the same time, the back of the truck filled with acrid black smoke and brightly coloured, lancing lights. A fearsome red-and-grey Dalek glided forth, chanting madly.

'You must obey! We will be obeyed! Resistance is useless, existence is useless, EXISTENCE IS – !'

The image vanished. The scene was proving too hard for Jack to play-act on his own.

The Mitchells were wheeling a fridge down the truck ramp, one brother going backwards with a sink plunger under his arm – for a brief glorious moment, the eyepiece of a Dalek.

Jack sneaked away, slipping through the two middle wires in the fence. He hurried into the wood of ghost gums, their shadows interlaced across the ground. When he emerged from cover, he could see the sun resting its head on the hills – primped pillows – its luxuriant hair tingeing their brown gold.

In the living room, Daniel finished screwing in the last light bulb that needed replacing and stepped down off the wooden stool. Simon, still panting from his run, was lying sweating on the rug in front of the wood-cased TV, watching *Skippy the Bush Kangaroo*. Daniel wondered if he should try to find Jack, but judging from what little light streamed in from outside, it would be too late for them to play now anyway.

He watched Jean enter from the kitchen, bone knives and forks in hand, to set about laying the table. Well, then, dinner was nearly ready, too; another reason it was too late to join Jack.

Jean glanced about the room. 'Simon, where's your brother?'

Simon picked at a blistered toe. 'Dunno.'

Daniel put the wooden stool back in the corner, where Jean liked it kept.

'He went for a walk, Jean.'

Jean placed folded beige napkins at the top of each plate. 'At night?'

It wasn't quite night yet, thought Daniel.

Jean put her now empty hands on her hips. 'I don't care how gifted he's meant to be; kids don't go out wandering at night.'

Daniel threw a look towards Simon, hoping Jean would understand. But either she didn't, or perhaps she wouldn't, for she kept up her insinuations.

Eventually, Daniel snapped, '*Please!*'

She desisted but still attempted to stare him down. Simon turned his face back to the TV, smirking. The news was now on and a footy player was scoring a goal to the evident delight of the newscaster.

Jack was in the Cunningham Casuarina that grew close to their house, straddling its wispy, faintly sticky branches smelling like pine. He'd climbed a fair way up and could see the lights on in the neighbour's house. The sun had buried itself below the horizon, but its faint glow still illuminated a purple sky.

Jack could hear his front door open. By the gentle way it swung, he could tell it was his father without looking.

A light went on in the neighbour's attic. Jack's house didn't have an attic. Jack thought an attic must be an exciting thing to have. He heard Daniel's footsteps lead up to the base of the tree.

'You'd better come inside, son.'

Daniel's face was framed between the needle-like foliage.

'Your show will be on soon,' he said.

With dinner over, Simon was the first to excuse himself from the table. He quickly threw himself on the orange shag carpet in front of the TV, switching it on and turning the channel knob till he found the football. Jack looked at his father as the two also excused themselves. Daniel nodded, walked over to the TV, and switched channels to the ABC.

The three-note insistent tune of *Doctor Who* was playing along to the image of a spiralling tunnel. Jack had to imagine what tints it was made of; only a couple of people in town had colour TVs.

Daniel stepped over Simon and sat next to Jack on the couch. Simon huffed, but didn't leave. He looked from the television to Jack before sitting up, figuring he could obscure Jack's view and get him that way.

'Simon, either lie down or watch it from here, with us,' said Daniel, pleasantly.

Simon grudgingly lay back down. Jack watched Jean get up from the table, dishes in hand.

'Aren't you going to watch it, Mum?' he asked hopefully.

Jean huffed, holding up the plates as if to indicate she had more pressing things to do.

'I'll help wash up after,' offered Jack.

Jean gave him a cynical flick of her head before disappearing into the kitchen.

Daniel smiled at Jack. 'Girls don't like science fiction, son.'

Jack turned his eyes back to the TV.

It was the most terrifying episode they'd watched yet. An ark in space, a mummified alien, a crewmate turning into a green … goodness knows what! Sarah Jane Smith was steadily becoming Jack's favourite *Doctor Who* sidekick. He remembered when she joined the doctor, in his previous regeneration, on that scary adventure set in the middle ages, involving those nightmarish Sontarans. All the fun and experiences she'd had since – not to mention the danger! – it made him envious.

Jack now knew just which door he'd enter if the doctor's TARDIS materialised outside his classroom the next day.

After Simon had tired of the show and left, he confided his wish to Daniel.

'Wouldn't that shake everyone up,' his father chuckled.

Chapter 3

It was recess and Jack was straddling the top row of a perpendicular iron grid. It formed part of the school's play equipment. It, and the other metal segments, had each been painted a different primary colour, but all were half peeled now, giving the whole a mottled look. The day was another scorcher, with not even a lone cloud in the sky, but at least this time he'd worn shorts.

Michael hadn't shown up to school today. Jack wondered if his absence was connected with Miss Jackson hitting him the day before.

He gazed down.

Noel was two rows below him on the five-row structure, looking through one of the squares like it was a window. Noel's pug nose was still his most distinctive feature, even when viewed from above.

For a brief second, Jack thought about trying to engage Noel in a game of their own making, but then he looked in the direction of Noel's gaze: the oval where Simon and his friends engaged in their favourite pastime, Red Rover. No, it wouldn't work. Although Noel would end up one of the last to get picked, he'd still rather play that than anything else. And, if he couldn't play, he'd watch.

Jack's eyes next roved over Emma and Kate who were on the swings made of old tyres. Kate had her same looped ponytails; Emma her hair out, long and dark. The two could have been sisters, except they hailed from different families on different sides of town. The Burnetts and Harrows respectively.

Jack caught Emma's eye.

'What ya doin', Jack?' she shouted, swinging back and forth.

He was startled. He couldn't remember Emma ever addressing him before, let alone to ask what he was up to.

Scrambling down to the row just above the ground, he carefully edged along it.

'Tryin' ta miss the crocs,' he explained.

The arc of Emma's swings lessened. Kate's, too.

'Where?' asked Emma.

Jack pointed at the bark-chip ground. 'There, in the water.'

Kate tossed her looped ponytails, like two oversized earrings. 'That's dirt, stupid.'

Jack was frustrated. 'No, it's not.'

He made his way to the opposite side of the grid, Noel looking down at him blankly. Jack leapt onto the monkey bars without touching the ground.

'Come on, Noel, ya gotta cross.'

Noel stared back, and it was as if Jack's invitation to play his game suddenly decided him to renew his attempt to join the other, on the oval.

'Nah, I'm playin' Red Rover.'

Jack climbed up the ladder of the monkey bars and was crawling across the horizontal one that bridged the two.

'No, come on, look, there's crocs.'

Noel plonked down onto the very spot the crocs were supposed to be wading (the dirt) and hurried towards the oval.

'Nah, seeya,' he shouted behind him.

To Jack's surprise, Emma and Kate had scaled the other side of the monkey bars to join him. He thought he'd show them by example how to get back on the grid and made the leap. With the fantasy of the crocs below dispelled by Noel, he came up with a new one.

'This is a web – I'm stuck!'

Jack turned to see that Emma and Kate, rather than following him, were instead hanging upside down on the monkey bars. He caught a glimpse of their white knickers and quickly turned away.

'Tryin' ta see down our dresses, Jack?' laughed Emma, pushing her tartan skirt up against gravity.

'No!' he shouted defensively.

Emma turned to Kate. 'What a pervert!'

The two giggled.

'I'm not,' he insisted, not even sure what the word meant. He climbed down a row so he was level with them. 'This is a web,' he explained patiently. 'Look, there's a spider.'

That got their attention. 'Where?' squealed Kate.

'Over there!'

Jack managed to pull his hand free of the sticky web (the bars of the grid) and hurry from a giant black hairy spider he could picture bearing down on him.

'Quick!' he shouted. 'He's coming to get us. Now I'm stuck!'

Emma and Kate became frightened, thinking there might be a real spider.

'Where? Where?' they chorused.

'There, there!' Jack echoed.

The girls dropped onto the dirt in a flap of dresses.

'Not there!' shouted Jack. 'That's the crocs.'

They jumped up and down in fright until it occurred to them there were no 'crocs'.

'You're a dick, Jacko,' said Emma.

Jack hated that name. It was what his classmates also called Miss Jackson. But in her case, behind her back.

'Jack!' he insisted, when Emma wouldn't let up.

First Emma, then Kate, walked away continuing to taunt him.

'Jacko, Jacko, Jacko ...'

He was glad when the two were out of hearing range. Climbing to the top of the navy blue grid, he sighed and surveyed his small world, beginning with the school.

There were the Federation Style red brick entrance building and offices, including Higgins'. Hidden behind them from the main road, the cheap portables. Next, the scuffed oval. Lastly, the play equipment he was now perched upon.

His eyes escaped the school grounds, skirting over the black pines and wire fence circling the oval and scampered up the main drag of Miller's Creek – unimaginatively named High Street.

Edging it, there was the butcher's with its green and white canvas awning where Jean would ask for 'nice pieces' of rump steak, and where Mr Gimbol (Michael's dad) would give him and Simon a slice of Fritz each. The hardware-cum-grocer's where Daniel might buy him and Simon a packet of mixed biscuits – six of this, six of that, in brown paper bags. A shoe shop where they would all go to be refitted every year, when they'd grown out of their last pair or worn them ragged. A greengrocer's, with its fresh fruit and vegetables, where his mum would shop and Mrs Holroyd would gift him and Simon a generous bunch of purple grapes. Next, a ladies' haberdashery – *Silco* – with its wooden reels of silk that rattled when unspooled

(Jean made her own clothes and some of his and Simon's as well). The tetchy Mr Sloane's record shop which had become, despite its proprietor, a cherished retreat of Daniel's. The newsagent's, with bound stacks of papers and magazines always sitting out the front, and the locale of Daniel's only bow to gambling: his weekly lottery ticket purchase. The pub, with its listing, tin veranda, where women were frowned upon, which made Jean angry, but which Daniel didn't seem to mind as he never went inside anyway.

A trip into town, especially with his mum, could be doubled, sometimes tripled, in length, as she knew everyone and they knew her; and for some reason they always found it necessary to discuss not just their own business, but everyone else's, too.

Jack's eyes next scaled Mount Miller itself, from whence the town derived its name. The remnants of a volcanic plug, its sides had been deemed too steep for grazing by the founding freeholders, and so it had never been cleared. Jack loved going up there with his father – they'd only been two or three times, unfortunately. But in the granite rubble at its base, rose several River Red Gums, as old as four or five hundred years, Daniel told him. They had existed even before white man reached the shores of Australia. 'What they must have seen,' Daniel would exclaim. 'What they've seen!'

Jack's gaze followed the winding and undulating road beyond Mount Miller that led to the front gate of his farm. His farm and house itself were obscured by the bare hill of the Harrow property.

This was Jack's world. He knew everyone in it and yet ... He felt alone. If only there was someone out there – a boy, given what his father had said the previous night about girls not liking science-fiction – whose imagination matched his own.

Jack's eyes by now had winged to the pale blue horizon, but they pulled up short again at the oval.

Noel had just been wrestled to the ground playing Red Rover. Simon, Troy and Adrian must have let him join in. He saw Noel get up, hugging his knee painfully and hopping off-field. Jack followed his progress but then spied something far more captivating.

Coming down the road that eventually joined the highway and wound its eager way to Adelaide and beyond, was a purple Valiant charger. Jack deftly shuffled along the top of the grid to the edge closest to the car, to get a better view of it racing into town.

Higgins was at his desk. Opposite him were Ms Jeffries and her daughter Mel.

He could only vaguely remember Juliet when she was a kid at the school. He was thirty at the time, beginning his first year of teaching, after ten spent in Adelaide trying to 'find himself'. He recalled Juliet's father had whisked her off to Europe when the mother was killed in that horrible accident.

Ms Jeffries still retained her Australian accent, but with the drawl absent, replaced by a refined and sophisticated cadence.

She really was a little too attractive, he decided.

Today she'd worn an Indian red crêpe ascot blouse with a mustard scooter skirt, ending well above her decidedly shapely knees. Her hair was pulled back in a tortoiseshell headband while around her slender neck she'd knotted a diaphanous orange scarf. If that wasn't provocative enough, on her feet were preposterously high platform shoes. For pity's sake, she already towered over him!

Her daughter seemed intent on her own fashion kick, of an opposite bent. A patchwork collared top – black, white and tan (yet sleeveless!), flared blue jeans (offensively ripped) and decidedly casual white and black Plimsolls (on which she appeared to have drawn).

As for the girl's hair ...

He refocused his attention on the mother. He tried calling her Mrs Jeffries but she insisted on 'Ms'.

'I'm not married, Mr Higgins.'

To make the point so blatantly when her own daughter sat beside her – Higgins could only wonder at such lack of discretion. He then tactfully insinuated her husband must have passed away (although that would still technically leave her a Mrs) but she persisted with an obscene obstinacy to claim that she wasn't married, never had married and probably now never would.

It was like she was unashamedly and wilfully bestowing on her daughter the title of bastard. To make matters worse, that 'bastard' did not seem in the least fussed that her own mother was so cavalier with her legitimacy. She, without shame, inspected every shelf in his office and every item on it.

At last, in a flap, he tried dropping the title altogether, but 'Jeffries' on its own was so masculine-sounding and the woman before him one of the most feminine and – damn it! – beautiful creatures he had seen, that tactic didn't work for him either.

He heard the sound of a car pulling up, with loud music blaring. Half glad of the distraction, he shuffled to the casement window, and was indignant to see the driver of a hideously purple Valiant practically pulling up on his front step.

'Um, excuse me, Mrs … er … um …'

The driver's door opened and a black pointed boot stepped out, belonging to a tall figure that rose up majestically. He seemed to take good note of Ms Jeffries' green Citroën. Meanwhile, Noel, still hobbling on his way to sick bay, stared adoringly at the Charger, his Red Rover tackle wounds momentarily forgotten. Higgins, emerging from the front entrance, darted a quick look at Noel disappearing inside before hurriedly surveying the astonishing figure standing before him. Just where had this outlandish creature hailed from? And why on Earth had he pulled up in the quiet, conservative town of Miller's Creek?

Jack observed all from his high vantage point atop the metal grid. He leaned forward, his interest fully piqued. There appeared to be a little misunderstanding before the man showed Higgins a letter. A scan of its contents seemed to clear things up, and the two men shook hands, turned and stepped towards the entrance.

Higgins' secretary, Pauline, was gently applying Betadine to Noel's knee. Pauline was the youngest adult working at the school. With frizzy red hair and a constellation of freckles on her cheeks, she was pretty, plump and beloved by all.

'Noel, I don't know why your teachers let you play that Red Rover,' she said, attaching a Band-Aid to the graze. 'If I had my way ...'

The door to the lobby flew open. Pauline and Noel looked up to see Higgins enter with a tall and, in Pauline's estimation, rather dashing young man.

'Ah, Miss Wheeler,' said Higgins to Pauline, 'meet Mr Rush.'

With a warm, inviting smile on his face, Rush took first Pauline's hand, then Noel's (who was surprised he was even included in the exchange), before giving Pauline a wink and breaking into a wonderful smile. She blushed red from her face to her extremities, even making a little sound of joy that Higgins immediately frowned upon.

Rush wore aquamarine velour bellbottoms, a paisley open-necked shirt and a black felt smoking jacket with large, mother-of-pearl cufflinks. His hair was of the darkest ebony, wavy, and rather long, and his skin was transparent and milky, which made his dark eyebrows, lashes and amber eyes all the more startling.

He was in his early thirties, but with a distinctly younger air. His accent was decidedly British, but not at all pompous. Pauline felt herself swooning.

There was an awkward pause, before Rush arched his imposing eyebrows at Higgins as if to say, 'What next?'

'So, um, yes, thanks for filling in at such short notice ...'

Rush merely smiled.

'Yes ... well,' mumbled Higgins, feeling he should add something further, 'it's only for six weeks, then our Miss Jackson will be back.'

Noel's ears perked up at this. A holiday from Miss Jackson – yippee! At that moment, the end-of-lunch bell sounded and Pauline told him that, since he was all patched up now, he should get to class.

Meanwhile, Higgins felt he should elaborate further on his need for a replacement teacher.

'She needed a rest,' he told Rush.

This time, Rush swapped his smile for a look of puzzlement. Higgins, realizing that he was perhaps revealing too much, was about to move on to another topic when he noticed Pauline, with her batting eyelids, intent on engaging Rush herself. Feeling that was somehow inappropriate, he beat her to it.

'I know Miller's Creek is small compared to what you're used to.' Higgins showed Pauline the letter. 'Mr Rush taught at Eton ...' Pauline mewed, impressed anew. 'But ... but?' Higgins, to his embarrassment, had forgotten why he had used that conjunction and to which clause he had intended to bridge it.

As he stammered nonsensically, Ms Jeffries and her daughter Mel exited his office.

Relieved, Higgins began to introduce both parties. 'But yes, I was about to say, you're not the only one starting today. We have a new student. This is her mother ... er ...' With that, he realised he'd stumbled straight into that embarrassing minefield of how to address her.

To his astonishment, Rush stepped in.

'Juliet Jeffries!' he beamed.

The two embraced in such a way that there could be no doubt they knew each other. It appeared even Juliet's own daughter was puzzled at such intimacy, for Mel looked up at her mum, wonderingly.

Juliet pulled away from Rush and smiled with a grateful air. 'You made it,' she half whispered to him.

'There was even a job going in town,' he jested.

'Oh, you didn't need to –'

'Nonsense. You'll find I haven't changed; I still hate to be idle.'

Higgins was annoyed at the exclusionary and intimate turn the conversation had taken and, without thinking, made a blustering sound.

Rush addressed him while still smiling at Ms Jeffries. 'Juliet and I met eleven years ago in Moscow. Juliet was performing *Prince Igor*. She is one of the world's greatest opera singers.'

Pauline cooed. Two exciting visitors to their town in one day! That's more than they'd had in ten years.

Higgins was less impressed, and conscious he had a school to run. 'Yes, well, the class will be waiting. Let me get you and Mel started.'

Higgins made his way to the door, then realised that not only was Rush failing to follow him, but the preposterous man had taken it upon himself to kneel before the girl!

'And you must be Mallika,' he said to her, looking strangely moved.

Mel curtseyed in response, then reached up to shake hands with the tall stranger.

Chapter 4

Jack was sitting on Miss Jackson's desk, drawing her geranium while the other kids were mucking about. They were still celebrating Noel's announcement that they had six weeks' respite from Miss Jackson.

The obverse of that *did* mean six weeks of Higgins, but although as priggish as Miss Jackson, he was certainly much less volatile.

Out of the corner of Jack's eye, he caught movement. At the end of the open-air corridor created by their portable and the one opposite, Jack could see Higgins with the man from the Valiant and, beside them, the lady and girl from yesterday, and possibly, in terms of the lady, from last night, too. The lady leant down, kissed the girl, and then departed. The three remaining approached class.

Jack resumed his seat – he had the details sketched in of the geranium anyway. The other kids were oblivious and continued to make a ruckus.

As Rush leafed through Miss Jackson's red notebook, filled with small, neat writing, Higgins kept a running commentary.

'After twenty-eight years here, Miss Jackson has got her syllabus pretty much down pat.' He tapped the notebook in Rush's hand. 'You'll find it all in there. She's got today's page marked.'

Mel lagged behind the two. She stopped abruptly and turned, staring straight through the window at Jack. The two immediately locked eyes in a way that made Jack gasp with a surprising recognition – for she was a stranger, after all. And yet she hadn't scanned about first but looked directly at him as though she not only expected him to be there, but – oddest thing of all – to be also looking out for *her*.

Mel could only be described as pixie-ish, with her long blonde hair. To Jack, she resembled one of those spritely creatures found in books brought to life by his favourite illustrator, Arthur Rackham. He'd never seen a girl with intricately braided and beaded hair before. Ever. She really did seem otherwordly. A line of poetry his father sometimes quoted came to him:

A fairy white, a woodland sprite,
An angel without wings

At the sound of Higgins impatiently calling her name, the girl glanced to her right and the spell was broken. Jack pressed his face to the glass to see that Higgins and Rush had paused on the steps leading into the corridor.

'Mel! This way.'

Mel winked at Jack before skipping over to Higgins. Rush stepped aside for her in a gentlemanly fashion. She followed Higgins inside while, curious, Rush paused to look inquisitively in the direction of her stare. The angle was too oblique from that standpoint, and the reflection on the window too glary, but he noted it was the last window at the back.

When the three entered class, the kids quickly divided up into boys down one side, girls the other.

Jack, suddenly shy, peered up only briefly from his drawing, worried the girl would hold his eye again, and gaze into him with that searching familiarity. But to his relief, she was instead engaged in scrutinising every corner of the room and was even giving the ceiling a thorough inspection!

Higgins cleared his throat. 'Good morning, children. This is Mr Rush.'

All of the students, with the exception of Jack, responded in sing-song.

'Good morning, Mr Rush.'

Rush was taken aback by their training but smiled. 'Why, thank you!' he bellowed, to show his appreciation.

Raising an eyebrow at Rush, Higgins went to speak but Rush beat him to it.

'And thank *you*, Mr Higgins.'

Higgins, flustered but not knowing quite what to do next, was forced to make a stumbling, hesitant and somewhat comical exit. Rush watched every painful part of Higgins' retreat before turning towards class.

'Ladies and gentlemen of distinction, this is your new classmate, Mel.'

Jack darted another quick look at Mel as Rush motioned to her to find a seat. It occurred to Jack the only one available was next to him on the boy's half, since Michael hadn't shown up. Hesitantly, the boys and girls watched in alarm as she took it. Jack and Mel examined each other, then Mel, Jack's drawing.

It showed a woman with a beak-like nose (the significance sadly lost on Mel) being swallowed whole by a giant, carnivorous geranium. Mel was impressed and signalled as much by beaming. From the front of class, Rush noticed her look of admiration but could only guess at what she'd seen. Jack, both self-conscious, and worried he'd be told off for doodling, quickly covered the picture with his exercise book. Rush's eyes, meanwhile, floated from the diorama to the posters of dinosaurs on the walls.

'So, my esteemed colleagues, I believe you're learning about oversized lizards.'

Rush turned to the clean blackboard, picked up a piece of white chalk, and started writing as he read from the notebook. Jack, feeling deflated for some reason, gaped out the window again.

'The Tyrannosaurus stood up to thirteen feet high and weighed seven tons. The Diplodocus stood sixteen feet high, was up to one hundred and eight feet long and weighed seventeen tons. The Stego ...'

Rush's voice trailed off. The kids glanced up from the notebooks they'd been busily scribbling in. Mel, who'd only managed to rule a very pretty margin and write down the heading of 'Dinosaurs', also stared upfront. Jack's focus remained outside.

Rush closed the notebook deliberately as if making a decision and turned to face the expectant class. He appraised them with a meditative look on his face, each one in turn.

'Now,' he began slowly, but quickly built up momentum, 'it seems to me that what this is really about is an exercise in *time travel.*'

Jack turned from the window in a flash. Mel's wide eyes travelled from him to Rush.

Discarding the notebook altogether, Rush began to pace. 'Now, it is very hard to picture the past, unless we bring our own experience to it. For instance, we might say that a

Tyrannosaurus was as heavy as two cars and as tall as three. Imagine something like that tearing down the street after you!'

Making a loud roar, the teacher ran several metres down the centre aisle, hands scissoring like jaws. The class laughed spontaneously before many cupped their mouths, worried they'd be told off for making a racket.

Rush proceeded to fill the blackboard with pictures rather than notes, all the while telling stories, making jokes, and venturing increasingly absurd and funny noises like dinosaurs might have made. He encouraged the kids to do the same, the more adventurous of them obliging.

Jack, a rare smile on his lips, took out his book again. Inspired by Rush's unorthodox teaching method, he saw he could attempt a new kind of drawing, more ambitious in scope. He set about it at once. Mel watched. Now and then, the teacher glanced over at him as well.

With a flourish, Rush drew one final stroke on the blackboard, the last of the worn-down chalk splintering to dust in his hand. The board was an abstract mess of lines and squiggles.

The end-of-school bell rang. For once, the class did not move.

Rush laughed. 'Well, off you go ... home time!'

The kids got up and scurried outside. Jack finished his drawing, closed his book and, not having been given homework, put it under his desk, being careful not to get a splinter under his nails. He dashed out after the other children, Mel following him. The charismatic teacher smiled at her as she passed. Then, when alone, he made his way to where she and Jack had been sitting.

Rush stood beside their desk, surprised at the intensity of feeling overwhelming him. Although energetic at all times, he had been particularly frenetic today, mostly, he imagined, to cover his nerves. To see this girl for the first time – this girl already eleven years old! – emotions whirled within him with nowhere to settle. He wondered about the boy next to her, how he'd moved from writing in one notebook, to scribbling in the next.

Rush gripped the desk giddily.

Never normally one to pry, curiosity got the better of his usually faultless ethics, and he reached under the desk and pulled out the boy's notebook.

'Wow,' he muttered.

The picture was a good likeness, a very good likeness indeed – in fact, more than that, a touch of magic. It was unmistakably of him, Rush, but dressed as Doctor Who in his present Tom Baker incarnation, emerging from the TARDIS.

The boy had drawn himself standing before the Doctor. Perhaps hoping to join the Time Lord in his travels? And there, peeping round the door of the TARDIS, captured in a mere few lines: Mel.

Rush peeked out the window in time to see Mel racing to catch up with Jack. Rush's focus dropped back down to the drawing.

There, underneath, a remarkable caption:

> *A fairy white, a woodland sprite,*
> *An angel without wings*

Jack unchained his bike.

'Hey, Jack is it?'

Jack appraised Mel shyly. She had the oddest accent, perhaps a mixture of the inflections of many countries, although it made a surprisingly musical mix.

'So, what do you do for fun round here, Jack?'

For a moment, Jack wondered if she meant at school, which would have been an odd question. But then he figured she must have meant living in Miller's Creek.

She certainly wasn't like the other girls, with their floral patterned dresses. Not in her trousers, like he'd wanted to wear that morning.

'Where are you from?'

'All over the world. Mum travels a lot.'

That explained the accent. They exited the front gate and walked beside the school fence in silence, Jack pushing his bike. He could sense her weighing him up. Here she was, having seen the world, and the furthest he'd been was into Adelaide. Jack struggled to say something as he stopped and got on his bike.

'Why come here then?' he asked, kicking at the pedals.

'Mum wants to revisit home. This is where she grew up. Plus the country air's meant to be better for her, the doctor reckons.'

Jack wanted to continue the conversation, but chickened out. He could see Emma's mum staring at Mel then at her own daughter in her pretty floral dress. It occurred to him they were looking at Mel the way some parents looked at him. Only her oddity was worn on the outside; his came through, no matter how hard he tried, in drips. Befriending her would only make him even more friendless. If it were possible to be *more* friendless.

Jack had wished only that morning he could have a friend to play with – a boy like himself – not a girl in trousers.

'Well, gotta go.'

As he pedalled off, Mel stepped after him. 'I liked your drawing!'

But Jack didn't turn back. Mel leant against the school fence. She caught a glimpse of Emma and Kate's mothers, Mrs Burnett and Mrs Harrow, staring at her. She waved and they turned away.

Chapter 5

As Jack arrived at the gate to the long dolomite road to his house, he realised he hadn't even looked for Simon's bike when fetching his. He hadn't seen him on the road home either, not that he ever got to pass Simon. Maybe he was at some training session or other. As Jack swung open the gate, he heard the sound of a car behind him.

Mel leaned forward on the ivory-coloured bench seat beside Juliet.

'Hey, Mum, Mum, stop!'

'What is it, Mel?' asked Juliet, more amused than startled.

'That's Jack – the one I told you about.'

What a delight, thought Mel, to be living next to that great artist. Juliet pulled over. Mel leaned out the window as Jack wheeled his bike through the gate.

'Jack, you live here?'

Jack pretended not to hear as he locked the gate. It was like this tomboy was deliberately following him!

'*Jack*!'

He reluctantly turned round.

'You live here?'

'Yeah.'

'We're just over there.'

The next-door neighbour's gate was wide open. Mystery solved. Jack felt a little deflated.

'We could give you a lift to school, couldn't we, Mum?'

'Yes,' said Juliet. 'Starting tomorrow morning, if you like, Jack?

Jack tried to smile.

The sky began to pale yawningly above the horizon. Above the silhouetted treetops, the morning star shone brightly one last time before it was washed out by day. The sun rose on Jack's house, and on the neighbours'. The cows were lowing in the field, rabbits scurried madly under fences, and lean foxes found their holes.

Mel and Juliet were hanging out washing.

Jean lowered her binoculars. Much of that laundry looked expensive and grand, in her opinion. She stepped away from the lounge-room window to appraise Daniel, Simon and Jack, who were having breakfast. She stared at Daniel, expecting him to ask what she had observed, but he did not look up from his toast.

'No sign of a husband,' she said, impatiently.

Daniel smeared his toast liberally with Vegemite. She expected such lack of taste from Jack. She put the binoculars back in their moulded, brown leather case, and tried to adopt a casual tone.

'She was your childhood sweetheart, wasn't she?'

Jack eyed his father sharply. Jean noticed and chided herself for the ring of hysteria in her voice as Daniel unfolded yesterday's paper and found something of urgent fascination within its pages.

'She won't remember me, darling.'

She plonked the binoculars case down hard on the table. Still he wouldn't look at her. Her gaze darted back to the neighbours' but she couldn't make out much through the prism of windows. Mrs Ashton had seen Juliet in town yesterday and said she was quite the most dreamy creature she'd ever seen pass through town, like a platinum blonde movie star. Jean pulled at her dark, slightly wavy do.

She remastered her even tone. 'All right, Jack, if they're so gracious as to offer you a lift, you'd better get going.'

Jack grabbed his bag and walked to the front door, but stopped and turned back to Simon.

'You coming, Simon?'

'Nuh.'

Jean waved Jack to the door. 'No, your brother's riding to school. He's got to build up his muscles for football. He's gonna be the success-story of this family, my Simon.'

Jean noticed Daniel's almost imperceptible wince, and felt an odd pang. Why couldn't she love him, or Jack, as she did Simon?

'Aw, Mum,' cooed Simon.

Daniel lowered his paper and peered at Jean as she stroked Simon's hair. No one seemed to notice Jack, who hesitated at the door.

'See ya, Dad,' he ventured.

Daniel slowly drew his eyes away from Jean. 'Okay, son.'

Jack looked again at Jean. She did not seem to notice him, or thought perhaps he had already left. As Jack went outside, he wondered at what his mother had mentioned.

Juliet, Daniel's childhood sweetheart?

Halfway through the long walk to the front gate, Simon sped past on his bike, making sure to half-brake and spin up the dust.

Mel and Juliet were waiting in the car. Simon had locked the gate. Jack clambered through the wires without opening it.

'Sorry I'm late, but I –'

'Hop in,' said Juliet, pleasantly.

Mel jumped out of the car. Jack slid in and Mel got back in beside him, the three occupying the front bench seat. Sandwiched between the two, he soon relaxed despite himself, and after a while felt oddly cosy. Juliet had a very subtle, fragrant smell. She wore a hat at an angle with a slight veil. Mel was in odd-looking jeans; she must have found them on one of her overseas adventures.

He found that Mel was smiling at him. He looked away shyly, not wanting her to think he was staring. She turned on the radio to the ABC. Some classical piece was playing.

Mel beamed knowingly at Jack. It was odd, this instant connection. He wondered what her imagination was like.

They pulled up outside school where Michael and Noel and a few other classmates were standing round, talking. They stopped to stare at the beetle-green Citroën. Mel got out and, to their surprise, Jack was next! Juliet drove away, giving a friendly toot, while Michael and Noel continued to gape at Jack and Mel. A flush spreading across his cheeks, Jack mumbled something unintelligible to Mel, before joining them. Mel stepped after him a pace, but hesitated when Jack cut her out of the circle by turning his back. Hurt, she half-ran, half-skipped to class.

Michael explained he was feeling better from his 'summer cold'. Jack wondered if he hadn't instead heard that Miss Jackson had left.

It struck Jack he *did* have a friend in Michael, and perhaps even in Noel.

They entered class, the three chatting. Their classmates were throwing paper planes, flicking rubber bands, and firing spitballs through biros from which they'd removed the nibs and ink tubes.

'... she just lives next door,' Jack was saying. 'So I thought ... Well, if I don't have to ride ...'

Mel was sitting alone at the front of class, in the boy's half. Jack shut his mouth and looked down sheepishly. Without peering up again, he found his usual seat at the back with Michael. Jack pulled from his knapsack the past year's *Doctor Who* almanac. Daniel had found it marked-down in the remainder bin outside the newsagent's, the only place in town to occasionally stock books.

For the last week, Jack had pored over its pages late into the night, reading and re-reading every word and picture caption, learning more about Cybermen, Sontarons, Daleks. He'd promised to bring it in for Michael.

Michael greedily thumbed through it, but was looking more at the pictures than reading.

Jack noticed a still in the almanac of the doctor half shielding Sarah Jane Smith, his ... the word came to him: companion. Travelling through time and space would be pretty boring and lonely on your own.

The rest of the class was still creating havoc ... except Mel. Guiltily, he tried to catch her eye but she wouldn't turn round and acknowledge him. He stared out the window; for once, not because he was looking for something better out there, but because he was feeling rather foolish.

Rush was strolling purposefully towards the portables, the sun gently draped around his shoulders like a cat, when he ran into Higgins, who seemed to be hanging outside the entrance door. Higgins ventured an awkward greeting.

'Morning.'

'Good morning,' returned Rush, reaching forward to push the door.

They entered the corridor and made their way to the homeroom. Before Rush could enter that, Higgins grabbed the doorhandle and held it closed.

'Everything well?' he asked.

Rush sized up Higgins, wondering what could be the matter. 'Yes,' he answered slowly.

Higgins cleared his throat. 'And Jack?'

So that was it: concern over a student. Rush stared through the glass at the boy he presumed to be Jack, the startling talent sitting by the window, and the only one apart from Mel to be quiet and contained amid the flurry and fury around them. He turned back to Higgins.

'The boy who's either drawing or staring out the window?' he clarified.

To Rush's surprise, Higgins grimaced. 'Well, not always,' he huffed.

Jack was still gazing out the window.

'Probably bored,' said Rush.

Higgins' jaw dropped. 'Bored?' he expostulated, once he'd got his mouth closed enough to form words. '*Bored*? At Miller's Creek Comprehensive?'

Rush inwardly sighed, but thought it best, outwardly, to placate. 'Well, Frank, sometimes if a student's particularly bright ...'

Higgins again flinched. 'Bored, Mr Rush?' he squawked. '*Here*? Where we offer the best a State School can – '

A duster crashed into the door's inset window, leaving behind a cloud of chalk particles. Higgins thrust his wide face against the glass, and Rush could only wonder that Higgins must have looked like a powdered clown from the other side.

Glen, standing nearest to the door, bent down to pick up the duster to relaunch it. But, as he rose, he saw Higgins' ghostly face framed in the glass. He swivelled round in panic.

'Mr Higgins!'

The kids madly scrambled to their seats as Higgins and Rush entered. Jack looked round vaguely at the clatter of desks and chairs. Michael moved the *Doctor Who* book from the top to the underside of the desk, resting it on his knees. Higgins surveyed the class sternly as Rush walked to the front desk, frowning, hoping Higgins would leave him to manage on his own. With not a soul making a squeak, Higgins nodded, self-satisfied, to Rush. But as he made his way to the door, he took a quick survey of Jack to make sure he wasn't proving Rush's thesis through staring out the window, and his eyes landed on Michael instead. The grubby boy was evidently oblivious to his presence, for he was busy reading under his table. Some rot, no doubt. Higgins began a slow, deliberate march towards him. Rush, glancing between the two, wished only that Higgins would quit the room, but could not think of a polite way of asking. He deliberated it was best to catch him up, which wasn't difficult given Higgins' slow-motion pace, all done for effect.

Mel watched the charade, her eyes meeting Jack's, as he turned from the window. Taking in what was about to happen, he immediately began elbowing Michael.

Higgins, with Rush nary a step behind, continued to advance along the row of desks.

'Michael ... *Michael*!' Jack whispered.

Higgins raised a finger to Jack, warning him not to alert his friend.

Michael craned up his head in time to see the shambolic figure of Higgins bearing down on him. Instinctively, he raised both arms as if to ward off a rock-fall. At the last second, Rush stepped between the two.

Higgins' face could not have formed a more eloquent expression of surprise.

'Michael!' announced Rush.

Michael reflectively shut the book with a thwack.

'Yes?' he squeaked.

The rest of the class was nervous, the exchange between Michael and Miss Jackson still raw in their memories.

Rush grinned. 'Whatever you've got there, it must be good if you have to read it under the table.'

Silence, then Jack heard a musical chuckle. He couldn't confirm that it was Mel, since Higgins and Rush obscured her from view, but it did have her tinkle and clarity. The class laughed a moment later, once Rush had joined her. Michael was perplexed; Higgins frowned. In a friendly fashion, Rush held out his hand. Jack immediately knew what for, and felt a flush of annoyance to know his book was about to be confiscated.

Gingerly, Michael handed it over. Flicking through its pages, Rush returned to the front of class, leaving Higgins in the back row like a student. Circling his desk, the teacher appeared utterly absorbed in the book. To Jack's infinite surprise, Rush began humming the opening bars from the *Doctor Who* theme, even playing up to it by pretending to flick an imaginary scarf.

The kids stared at him tentatively. Mel smiled, then glanced over her left shoulder to pick out Jack. Their eyes met. He smiled in a way that he hoped conveyed his apology. Rush looked up from the almanac.

'Jon Pertwee was an excellent Doctor, but the current one … yes, yes, he's very good. The Daleks versus the Cybermen? The Daleks every time. Now, who is that new Doctor?'

'Tom Baker, sir.'

It was Jack's turn to stare open-mouthed. Mel had answered Rush's question.

'Tom Baker, yes!' shouted Rush, swivelling round but directing his words at Higgins. And then, to Mel, more quietly, 'Thank you, Mel.'

Jack remained fixated on Mel, his forehead creasing. Sneaking another look back over her shoulder, she smiled again, as if to say, Well, didn't *you* know that? Jack grinned in return. With her plucky self-assurance, she really was quite unlike the other girls. Or boys, for that matter.

Rush had his nose back in the almanac and was walking down the aisle toward Jack and Michael's desk. He stopped in front of it.

'Ah, Doctor Who, travelling through time and space. Did you know, Michael, that you can travel in time through music?'

'Nuh.'

Rush looked up from the almanac, before pirouetting to face Higgins. 'Well, leastways you can travel backwards!'

Higgins' eyebrows hit his hairline. Rush made his way back to his desk, whereupon he began circling it once more.

'The Kinks' *Lola* was an unfortunate romance I had in Bristol; Mahler's *Symphony No. 5*, an interminable convalescence I underwent in a sanatorium on the Bay of Islands; and, eleven years ago now, Borodin's *Polovtsian Dances* ...'

Mel wrote down that last piece, thinking her mother might know it. When she looked up, Rush was regarding her meaningfully.

'... was ...' he uncharacteristically mumbled, seemingly now engaged in a conversation with himself. 'Well, maybe the best choice I ever made.'

Mel was pleasantly puzzled, the others kids unsure of these ramblings. To Higgins, such carryings-on smacked of an unorthodoxy to which he would have to give weighty consideration. A scene would achieve nothing now. He walked awkwardly towards the door.

As he passed Mel, she blurted out a question. 'Mr Rush, can *we* travel in time?'

Higgins hesitated.

'Yes, of course!' Rush announced, breaking out of his private thoughts. He then glanced at Higgins mischievously. 'But it helps with the curtains shut!'

Rush lunged at the closest window hangings and drew them closed. He nodded to the kids to do likewise with those still drawn. In pairs, they stood on their desks and pulled the rest shut in something of a Mexican Wave. Higgins looked round, dismayed. With the closing of the last curtains, Higgins felt the light drain off his face.

To everyone else, the denuded atmosphere was more velvety, more wondrous; to Higgins, shadowy, suspicious. Rush gave him a wink before beginning a strange narration.

'In a dimly lit but stately drawing room in Salzburg, Austria, Leopold Mozart …' Rush grabbed Higgins by the shoulders, shoving him down in the teacher's chair '… sits and listens to his talented daughter Nannerl …' Rush pointed at Mel '… playing on the harpsichord.'

Rush led Mel gently to the front desk, placing her fingers on top of it as though it were a harpsichord. She promptly realised what he wished her to mime, and got into the spirit of the thing by striking a musician's pose.

'Leopold,' Rush continued, nodding at Higgins, 'has great hopes that one day Nannerl will perform for distinguished audiences throughout Europe.'

Higgins had had about enough and rose. Rush pushed him back down in his chair.

'Leopold is a musician and violinist of some note himself,' said Rush to Higgins. 'He is Nannerl's stern and exacting teacher. The year is 1762.'

As Rush described more of the scene, Jack came to see Higgins dressed in a high-parted, curled grey wig, with coat, jacket and breeches in a deep royal blue, trimmed with gold braid. Mel he pictured attired in a crimson pelisse, plainly embroidered in black swirls. The room became a voluptuous profusion of thick gilded mouldings, weighty brocades, and abundant marbling – in short, all the wonderful excesses of the Baroque era.

Mel played a ditty at the pretty harpsichord, lacquered as it was in paper printed with elaborate patterns. Rush strode over to Jack. Nervous, Jack wanted to slide under his desk, but Rush gestured to him. The next thing he knew, he was at the front of class, part of the historical play-acting.

'Meanwhile,' Rush continued to narrate, 'little Amadeus, who has been sitting fidgeting, looking out the window ...'

The class laughed. Jack tried not to blush.

'... listening to his sister play, can no longer contain himself.'

Jack, imagining himself now clothed in a gold figured waistcoat and wearing a bicorne hat, began picking out tunes on the harpsichord as Nannerl tried to continue her practice.

'Nannerl,' narrated Rush, 'turns to Leopold, pouting.'

'Papa!' yelled Mel. 'Tell Amadeus to go outside.'

Rush put his hands on Higgins' shoulders, preventing him from rising. 'Leopold sits up straighter and says, "Amadeus, don't disturb your sister. Go outside and play."'

Rush let go of Higgins' shoulders and began to weave between his three actors.

'As Leopold speaks,' Rush continued, 'Amadeus moves to the other side of the harpsichord and again picks out his tune.'

Jack echoed the direction.

'But Leopold growls: "Amadeus!"'

Jack jumped, startled, and moved away from the desk. Mel made a face at him as she reclaimed her seat.

'But little Amadeus does not want to go outside and play,' said Rush. 'He is fascinated by the harpsichord and keen to show his father his own tentative attempts to compose music.'

Jack nervously held up a dirty manuscript (his book of drawings) to Higgins.

'Papa, look at my music.'

'Leopold was gruff,' narrated Rush, 'as he snatched the book. "What's this?" he mumbled. "What are you trying to do here?"'

Higgins reluctantly glanced over Jack's exercise book.

'Leopold looks at the messy manuscript and childish notations and sighs with agitation.

'"Why don't you go outside and play?" asks Leopold. "I'm listening to Nannerl. We'll start serious lessons for you soon enough."'

Rush shook a finger at Higgins. 'But Leopold's eyes and mind are drawn back to his young son's notes and an idea begins to form in his head.'

Higgins sat up straight.

'"Amadeus! From where did you copy this?"'

Rush slammed the desk in front of Higgins. 'No, not a suspicion of plagiarism!' he yelled. 'Something else!'

For the first time, Higgins joined in the play-acting. 'Oh, yes, yes, quite. Amadeus, Amadeus, come back inside. Go to the harpsichord and play your composition for me. Nannerl, move aside for your brother, please.'

Mel trotted off in a huff, glancing back at Jack. He poked his tongue out at her, before sitting back down at the desk, and throwing out imaginary coattails behind him.

'Mozart plays his *Alla Turka*, quickly livening to its military band rhythms,' intoned Rush while throwing up his arms, as if conducting. 'Leopold is amazed by the little boy's composition. Not only does he have a talented daughter but a son who is a child genius!'

The-end-of-school bell sounded just as Jack passionately struck the last ecstatic note, before raising his fingers off the harpsichord.

Jack turned to see Rush, Higgins and the entire class staring at him. At once he was plain Jack again, sitting in a darkened classroom where he had been thumping on the teacher's desk.

Rush nodded expansively at Higgins, as if to say, 'There! He's coming out of his shell.'

Higgins could only manage a grunt.

Mel caught up with Jack at the school gate.

'You were brilliant!' she cried.

Jack felt himself turning red, and fumbled with the strap on his bag.

'I ... well ...'

Mel simply grabbed his arm, pushing him forward and into Juliet's awaiting Citroën.

Juliet drove up to Jack's gate and parked, expectantly. Jack clambered over Mel to get out. This time, rather than climb through the gate, he leapt over it instead. Juliet wound down her window.

'Aren't you going to open the gate, Jack?'

Jack looked down shyly. Jean was probably home and he wondered if she would like visitors when she wasn't expecting any. She'd be worried the house wasn't clean.

'It's a long way to walk,' added Juliet.

He hoisted his bag to his shoulder. 'It's all right.'

Mel clambered over her mum to stick her head out the window.

'Why don't you come to our place, Jack?

Juliet nodded assent.

'Yes, why don't you?'

Jack wanted to, but his parents would be expecting him. He didn't think Daniel would mind, but …

'No, no, I think I'd better be getting home.'

He turned quickly, before either of them could make further entreaties, and got away, thrusting his hands deep into his pockets. As he dragged his feet, he noticed the runnels edging the road. Pulling his hands from his pockets, he picked up a broken bit where it was eroding and threw it like it was a grenade. When it hit the ground and blew up in dust, he made the appropriate sound of an explosion.

Jack noted the driveway was getting quite rough, with all the potholes and fissures. Just another of Daniel's jobs he hadn't done, according to Jean – getting a truck loaded with gravel to fill them.

He heard a beep and looked off to his left to see the green Citroën through the fence and line of poplars. Mel appeared to be sitting on her mum's lap, steering. Jack lowered his hand with his next 'bomb' in it. His shyness had returned and he felt a total fool next to this girl who could drive, and wondered why that should matter to him.

Chapter 6

Neither his mum's Ford nor his dad's Holden station wagon were parked under the veranda. Simon's flash red bike was missing, too. The only vehicle was his rickety green bike. Jack went inside.

Even though he had no expectation anyone would be home, he called through all the doors adjoining the living room.

'Dad? Simon? Mum?'

He went to the fridge to fix himself a bowl of Rice Bubbles, and found a note stuck to it with a magnet. It was in his dad's handwriting.

Your Mum and I have gone to watch Simon at footy practice.
Dad
P.S. Tea's in the fridge.

Jack looked inside the fridge to find a TV meal in its foil container. He didn't feel hungry. He went to the front veranda and stared up at the hill where Juliet and Mel's house was obscured by trees.

Juliet was working in the garden, a straw hat on her head and big white gloves on her hands. She carried a trowel in her right.

'Jack!'

'I can go,' he said, quickly.

Juliet got to her feet, dusting her hands and knees of dirt.

'No, don't be silly,' she laughed. 'Mel's in the Cubby House.'

Juliet nodded to a structure on stilts some distance off. Jack knew the structure without having to turn. He'd been near it but never inside. The Cubby House was a corrugated iron room raised up on six treated pine posts, with a balcony at one end. A huge gum tree hugged the whole with its octopus arms. Underneath lay a great log, upon which someone had piled bones: cows, sheep, foxes, snakes, rats; you name it. Jack had always wondered how to get inside. He thought Mel very brave to go in there alone.

He approached the closest he ever had, and discovered a trapdoor underneath.

'Mel?'

He called out again, to no avail. Just as he turned to leave, he saw a rope ladder thrown down, nearly making him jump.

'Jack, it's you! Come up.'

Although he'd never climbed one before, he knew from *The Six Million Dollar Man* it was easier sideways, and got the hang of it quickly enough.

The trapdoor opened up under a low bench, which Jack then had to crawl out from under. He figured the bench was probably there to stop people falling down the hole. For some reason, Jack thought it was the kind of clever thing his dad would think to do. Even though his mum said he never got much done, when he did fix or make things, he did them extremely well.

Rising up beside the bench, Jack observed it had a double purpose. Climbing onto the bench would mean you could push your way up through the ceiling hatch and get on the roof, no doubt. Wow! It really was cleverly designed. Why had he ever been scared of the place? He started scrambling onto the bench, hardly able to wait to check out the view that he knew would overlook the valley and his own house, when Mel called out.

Jack saw there were two open doorways leading from the room he was in. One led to the empty balcony; taking the other, he stepped into a sparsely furnished room, covered in wax paper with crayon drawings all over it, rather neat. Mel was lying on a quilted doona, listening to something through her earphones. To Jack's surprise, he realised the place must have electricity.

He plonked down next to her. She held the big rubber earphones towards him.

'Jack, you've *got* to listen to this. Quick, it's on the radio.

Mel leant close to Jack so that they could both listen in. The music was a strange dance of flute and oboe, backed by an orchestra, like two birds trying to fly directly upwards, but only succeeding in a majestic hovering.

Mel smiled at the delight on Jack's face. 'I'd love to wake up to a morning as beautiful as that,' she said.

Jack frowned. 'Morning? It's just music.'

Mel straightened in horror.

'Just music! Weren't you listening to Mr Rush?'

Jack nodded slowly. The music was swelling now, as from the sort of joy he'd never known. Those birds would never quite succeed in their vertical lift, but there was a beauty and choreography in their striving.

'Yes, but how can music be *about* anything?' he asked, still a little sceptical, despite the images that Mel's words, in conjunction with the music, had conjured in his mind's eye.

'Well, of course it can,' insisted Mel. 'Listen.'

The two leant in close to the one headphone. Even their breaths were mingled. He'd never been so close to a girl before.

Her smell was like cut grass. The music died down, only to hint at rising again.

Mel stared at Jack intently. 'That's not your average morning: jumping out of bed, feeling horrible, going off to school tired.'

'What sort of morning is it, then?' he asked, gazing into her green eyes.

'Well, it's early, still early, but it's pleasant. Listen, that's the sun coming over the hill, and the sound of birds, not traffic. There! Hear that, the trilling? It's beautiful. A slow awakening. A day full of promise!'

A smile of vague understanding spread over Jack's face. Music had made him see things before but he thought that was always what *he'd* evoked. But perhaps, just perhaps, the musician could make you see things of their own devising, too. He blinked at Mel. At last, he wasn't afraid for her to look so long into his eyes, nor of himself looking into hers. Perhaps there, finally, was that connection he'd always longed for, that friend with whom he could play on equal footing. That … *companion* with whom to travel in time and space. She was searching him just as thoroughly, and for the first time he really wondered what was going on in another's head. Juliet's voice at the manhole interrupted the moment.

'Mel?'

Mel jumped up, roughly putting both headphones over his ears, laughing at his protestations, and bumbling to the balcony.

'Yes, Mum?' she called, leaning over the railing.

The music ended, replaced by the dulcet tones of a male announcer: 'And that, of course, was the *Morning Mood* movement of the *Peer Gynt* Suite by –'

Mel yelled at Jack to join her. Jack pulled off the headphones and hurriedly looked around for a pen and paper to write on. He spotted the crêpe paper Mel had been drawing on and quickly scribbled down the name of the piece and what he thought was the composer – Mel had shouted over the name.

'Do you want to ask if Jack would like to stay for tea, honey?' Juliet's voice rose up from below.

'He'll stay, Mum.'

'Think you should ask first?'

Jack quickly thrust the paper inside his pocket as Mel pirouetted and skipped back into the room.

'Jack, Mum wants to know if you're staying for tea?'

Jack realised his parents would be home by now, and most likely concerned for him.

'Really, I should be getting – '

Mel cut him off, providing the answer he wanted to give.

'I said yes.'

He was a little worried but answered with a smile.

Jack had peered through the windows to Juliet and Mel's house over the years but never entered. That would have meant breaking in, of course, and overcoming his natural reluctance. From what he'd gleaned, though, the place seemed like a shrine. Actually getting beyond the seal and surveying its innards, that impression was strengthened. It was the exact antithesis to his own home. Jean liked everything clean and modern. She hated any kind of mess or clutter. There was an awful amount of clutter in Juliet's house, though Jack wouldn't have said it was messy. There were instruments galore, a piano with candlestick holders; a veritable antique's store. Entering it finally, made him think of Howard Carter discovering Tutankhamun's tomb unplundered. Just how had Juliet's house avoided being ransacked? Come to think of it, Daniel had kept a pretty close eye on it.

Jack always thought good people would come home to it. Although he didn't know it was *their* house, then.

The place smelt different to home, too. Home smelt clean. Just that: clean. But this home smelt of *things*, of herbs, of wool, of must, of dust, of flowers and dried eucalypt leaves, and expensive, pungent perfumes. It was a testament to Juliet's industry that the place had come so alive during such short reoccupation, as if water had been thrown on a seed, and sunlight let in to shape it upwards.

'I rang your house,' she told Jack, as she put on a record. 'But no one answered.'

Jack explained why.

'I thought football was a winter pastime?'

When Jack screwed up his nose, Juliet chortled. 'Don't worry, I understand. It's a perennial obsession. Sport is our national religion.' She then sighed theatrically, as she turned up the volume on the record player. 'Ah, if only the arts inspired the same fervour.'

Debussy's *Prelude to the Afternoon of a Faun* brought the dining room to life with its strange nostalgia, rich with sensuality and finesse. Jack never thought the flute sounded so intoxicating – a far cry from the ubiquitous squeaking recorders at school.

Tantalising aromas emanating from the kitchen soon overtook the unfamiliar smells of the house. Jack and Mel set the table, and Jack was given the seat at the head. With a little flourish, Juliet placed a meal of *Coq au Vin* in front of their visitor. Jack looked at it queerly. Mel glanced at her mum in concern. The taste was different to the plain meat-and-three-veg he was used to, but he savoured its richness and thick, syrupy texture. He smiled at the others and they smiled in turn as Juliet sat down, relieved.

They ate by candlelight, something Daniel and Jean only did when there was a power blackout. Juliet, her radiant face lit with the flickering, guttering light, finished off a nearly empty bottle of Babycham while he and Mel drank orange juice, and Juliet talked about how she would barely fit into the Cubby House now. Once it had seemed so big to her. Daniel had done a splendid job, though. Ah, thought Jack, he was right! It *was* Daniel's handiwork.

Juliet said the Cubby House was the opposite of the TARDIS, smaller on the inside than it ought to be. Now, it left her feeling like Alice from Lewis Carroll, a big kid in a world grown suddenly tiny.

Black Forest gateau was dessert – again, a far richer, refreshing and moist sponge cake than the plain ones Jean would sometimes bake.

When dessert was eaten and the three had washed up, they retired to the couches, already occupied with abundant pillows and throws. Jack was feeling deliriously tired but in a dreamy, pleasant fashion.

Juliet abruptly changed tone, and looked at Jack strangely as if trying to find another face in his, the shadow of an influence, or impression left from the mould.

She took a sip of her tumbler of Tokay, the Babycham drunk and left to roll under the fringed couch.

'Jack, Mel tells me you're quite the artist.'

He threw a glance at Mel, embarrassed. Not many people seemed to like that he drew. Mel nodded it was okay.

Juliet folded her legs under her on the couch, and said in a knowing tone, 'Who do you inherit that talent from?'

'Dad's a painter.'

Juliet was obviously interested, and oddly relieved. 'Oh good, I'm glad he kept at it. Landscapes ... portraits?'

Jack was confused. Juliet leant over to place her empty tumbler on the coffee table.

'Houses,' he mumbled.

Something stopped Juliet dead. There was a slightly awkward pause. Mel took the tumbler and lowered it the five centimetres to the table before rolling her eyes at her mum. Juliet seemed pained. Mel broke the silence.

'Mum, today Mr Rush said his favourite piece was *Polovtsian Dances*. Have we got that?'

'I'm so glad you like Mr Rush,' said Juliet, unexpectedly serious.

Mel matched her intensity. 'Why?'

Juliet animated back to life, getting off the couch.

'Have we got *Polovtsian Dances* indeed! We should do! That's where we met.'

Juliet thumbed her extensive collection of records.

'*Polovtsian Dances* is from the opera *Prince Igor*. I once performed it in Moscow, my nod to *glasnost*...'

Jack looked perplexed. Juliet noticed and reached for a photograph on the piano. She handed it to him. It showed the oddest structure, like something from Disney, all onion spires in multiple colours.

'Saint Basil's Cathedral in Red Square, Moscow,' she told him.

Juliet set down the needle and the tune came to life, the notes twirling in a sumptuous dance. Soon it evolved into a sparkling procession, a vigorous tumbling acrobatic display. Again, like the Debussy piece, it relied on woodwind, which sculpted an arching, repetitive, melodic contour before breaking into a terrifically clamorous cacophony of pure ... well ... noise.

Mel, dancing in a freeform manner, grabbed Jack. He joined in, tentatively, though he didn't really know how.

Also on her feet, Juliet hummed along to the music. Pirouetting ever faster, without warning she crashed into the record player. Her hands flew up to her face and she closed her eyes, rocking slightly and wincing in pain. Mel let go of Jack and lifted up the record arm.

'Are you all right, Mum?'

'I'm dizzy. Very dizzy.'

Jack looked at Mel worriedly.

Chapter 7

The moon was out, looking dishy. Jack and Mel were sitting on the fence that separated their properties, watching the sky for shooting stars.

In Jack's head, he could still hear the theme of *Polovtsian Dances* as an echo, as if it were dying out in the pinpricked cauldron of night.

'Well, better be off,' he said at last, hopping off the treated pine railing and onto the languid grass.

Mel was still staring above. After a brief pause, she sighed, 'I'll walk you to the stile.'

They wandered further down the fence line, Mel running a hand along the sagging wires. Jack looked down the valley at his house. Jean's Ford pulled up, the high beams on. They flicked off. Out she got, followed by Daniel and Simon. Jack kicked himself for not getting back earlier. Now he would have to answer his mother's questions. He watched them stroll to the front door, probably wondering why no lights were on inside. Simon went in first, after dumping his mud-caked boots on the rubber entrance mat, followed by Jean who fussed over him, and lastly Daniel who glanced up briefly at the hill before closing the door behind him.

There was no way in the dimness Daniel could have seen them.

Now that his family had beaten him home, Jack no longer wanted to join them. He was as happy as he had ever been, in the outdoors. More so now, because he was accompanied.

Mel jumped up, trying to pull a gumnut off a low branch of a ficifolia. Almost at once, he worried that this moment – which he was sinking into as if into the most comfortable, sweet-smelling hay – was of excruciating dullness to a girl who'd seen more of the world in her tender eleven years than the townsfolk of Miller's Creek combined.

'Must be pretty boring here?' he queried, his uninvited dejection worsening.

She finally got her gumnut, yanking it off as the branch flew back up as irritably as the swish of a horse's tail, and just as noisy. She looked at him funny.

'Being a city girl, I mean.'

Mel turned, surveying the timeless arc of the blueing hills, digesting his meaning.

'It's lonely,' she answered at last, in an oddly flat tone. 'Even the trees are lonely.'

She nodded in slow motion, mirroring the rhythm of a nearby tree sapling, standing isolated. Jack noted the wire barrel staked round its trunk. Could only have been his father's work. Without that protection, it would never have survived the cropping of the sheep.

Mel's throat moved strangely, like she was swallowing nervously. The whole sky and land went a hue darker.

'If I ...' she stumbled, then admitted the word, '*died* here, though, the trees would have me for company.'

Jack could no longer see her expression, only the outline of her hair, which she'd pinned up in an almost boyish do. What was the meaning in those words, the sudden change of tone in someone he had so far found ebullient, carefree? Before he could ponder the question further, he heard his father calling.

Daniel had stepped out onto the front lawn, and was looking around in an alarmed fashion.

'Where's *your* dad, Mel?' Jack asked, finding his own voice and tone had subdued with the purpling sky and dimming landscape.

Perhaps because she realised her mood had infected his, she 'came to', and adopted a lighter tone and mien.

'Dad? Oh, well, he's … I shouldn't tell, but he's MI6.'

'MI6?' he queried, feeling ignorant and unsophisticated once more next to this seasoned connoisseur of the world.

Mel adopted a shooting pose, like Roger Moore as James Bond in those distinctive opening titles prefacing the films.

'Secret Intelligence Service. He's a *spy*.'

Jack thought about this for a second. His history teacher would often rabbit on about those dangerous commies under Brezhnev.

'For us?' he asked in a hurry.

Mel laughed. Her features were coming back to Jack, as his eyes adjusted to the night and the stars grew brighter.

'Yes, of course, silly,' she laughed, doing a pirouette. 'But he's so secret not even Mum's allowed to know where he is.'

Something in this did not quite tally for Jack. With Mel's reference to the tree's loneliness, that was like he imperfectly understood, and she was unable to perfectly impart. But with these revelations, it was like she was holding back, not quite giving him the full picture.

'But if he's ...' Jack began, trying to put his doubt into words.

Mel seemed uncomfortable. To cover, she playfully tapped him on the arm. 'You're it!'

'What?' asked Jack, genuinely confused at her meaning.

She beheld him like he was a simpleton. 'Hide and seek!'

She ducked behind the large tree she had only minutes before been stripping of gum nuts. Jack shook his head slightly (he was enjoying talking, really talking), but at last decided to join her in her game and walked behind its crusted bole.

To his infinite surprise, she wasn't behind it! He did a quick circle of the trunk, in case she was niftily keeping him exactly opposite.

No, she definitely wasn't there.

He heard the sound of his front door shut. He glanced back at his house; Daniel must have gone back inside.

A movement in the corner of his eye caused him to turn around. Mel was peeping from behind one of the ghost gums that were situated further back up the hill towards her house, where they grew thickly.

How on earth had she suddenly got up there?

She ducked behind it. Her heard her voice a moment later, oddly echoing.

'Don't give up, Jack.'

He ran up to the ghost gum only to find that she had disappeared from behind that too!

He scanned the others in the clump.

'Mel? Mel, where are you?'

Jack stopped calling when he heard his father calling him in turn.

'Jack! Jack!'

Daniel had retrieved a Dolphin torch and was wandering up the hill, the light bobbing about in the grass.

Jack hesitated a second, had one more look around, then jumped the stile and ran down the hill to join his father.

After dinner, when Jack was helping Daniel fix the leaky washing machine which had been moved to the shed, he asked him about that line of poetry.

Daniel took a while to understand, but then finally looked up with his washed-out blue eyes. Jack wondered if they'd ever been as startling as his own, or always that diluted.

'What line, son?'

Jack felt a sudden acute embarrassment but muttered it all the same.

'A fairy white, a woodland sprite, an angel without wings.'

Daniel rubbed the grease off his fingers, as if they were suddenly of infinite fascination to him. When he did look up again, it was ruefully.

'Oh, that's nothing. I made that up, Jack.'

Daniel got up and walked to a half-stripped cupboard in the corner. He pulled out a musty box and took from it a record.

'Maybe I should introduce you to some music myself. I used to play this band to death.'

Retrieving a record player from the same cupboard, Daniel set it down on the workbench and lifted the dusty cover. He placed the record on the wheel, and set it spinning. The needle dropped into its trench, and so began a long, aching, musical sigh.

''Waterloo Sunset' by the Kinks,' beamed Daniel, enjoying the look of amazement on his son's face.

The chords tumbled in an inexorable pitiless resignation, creating a feeling in Jack almost beyond his comprehension till his father put it in a word that he perceived would forever reverberate with him, as if tuned to the timbre of his own soul.

'*Melancholy*. The Kinks are best described as *melancholy*.'

The tune then assumed a haunting quality, a strain of hesitancy, as the singer sang, 'But I don't need no friends. As long as I gaze on Waterloo Sunset, I am in paradise.'

It became combative once more, the loss, if not totally forgotten, then relegated to the bittersweet. Oddly, the piece for Jack evoked that overgrown garden in the roofless settler's house.

'Why do you like it, Dad, if it makes you feel sad?'

Daniel regarded the buttressed ceiling of the shed. 'Sometimes it's okay to feel sad, if it helps you remember someone.'

Jean was doing the last of the ironing, getting Jack and Simon's clothes ready for the morning. She packed up the ironing board and put it in the cupboard, then wandered to the window. Until recently, night had always been dark outside – their nearest neighbours, the Harrows, were a couple of kilometres away and obscured behind a copse of pine at that – but tonight there were two stars of habitation in the sky. Light emanated from the shed where Daniel and Jack were up to goodness knows what, and then there was that more distant satellite up on the hill, signalling the presence of that woman and her daughter.

How Jean had wished – wished again and over – for her isolation to be lessened. How she ached to have a home in town. Daniel wasn't the social gadfly she was and had difficulty making friends. Traits echoed in Jack. Just a few weeks back she'd taken Daniel to one of her dos in Miller's Creek, because Mrs Saunders' husband was also present. (Although he had an excuse to be hanging out with the women: work injury.) Daniel barely spoke, yet was attentive with tea and cakes until the topic got on to that dreadful Whitlam and his appalling policies.

Of all the times Daniel could have chosen to speak, it was then.

'I like him,' he'd rambled, silencing the room as he balanced a silver tray of macaroons. 'He has something extremely rare for a politician ... vision.'

Jean had distracted the ladies with some irrelevancy or other, but the words were out. She and her circle had venerated Australia's former Prime Minister bar one, Menzies. But perhaps Daniel had never forgiven Menzies for the man's war mania. Daniel had served two terms in Vietnam.

It was 1967 when he got embroiled in it; they'd been together seven years. Simon was six, Jack three. Daniel was working as a mechanic fixing planes at the nearby RAF base. He'd joined the reserves after unsubtle pressure that it would mean keeping his job. The colonel knew about the mortgage on the farm – a result of Daniel's father's drinking and debts – and said if he signed up proper, he'd be made a private and stationed out to repair work in Nauru for a year. He'd then be set up with an ex-pat's loan to regain ownership of his family property.

Jean had been keen on the idea – she wondered vaguely if she'd admire him more if he were in uniform. Daniel had eventually agreed against his better judgement. Six months later, the promise broken, he was in Vietnam, stationed at the US airbase in Khe Sanh, site of one of the bloodiest battles of the war.

He had never spoken about it, except to ask Jean to refrain from mentioning it to their kids, which she felt was akin to siding with the hippies. Quiet and reserved before, he had returned home with a taciturnity bordering on catatonia.

They'd staved off the banks with their war-loan but Daniel hadn't turned out much of a farmer, unable to give up his sheep to the knackery and only selling their wool. Before long, he had to supplement their income by painting houses. To Jean's great mortification, people would make jokes of his ewes. 'Yous with your ewes.'

Because he was away most days, John Harrow took care of much of the management of their sheep, seeing to docking, mulesing and shearing, and pocketing half the profits.

Jean traced the outline of the neighbour's property on the glass.

That light on the hill had come finally, but it was not the ship in the night she hoped for, but something far more troubling, more enigmatic. The queasy possibility occurred to her that had never struck before: that she might lose a husband she could never claimed to have properly owned.

Jack, with teeth brushed, dressed in pyjamas, and snug in bed, was trying to drift off to sleep. He usually liked to go to the bottom of his bed, turn around, and then make his way back as if from the mouth of a whale, all without untucking the bed. But tonight he was pretending not to speculate just who 'Waterloo Sunset' reminded Daniel of.

For he knew.

Chapter 8

The first thing Jack saw when he opened his eyes was a fox walking past his window. It stopped, and the two stared at each other. When the fox broke its gaze and fleet-footed it, Jack sat up abruptly, with an abortive, almost guttural, cry.

Still heavy with sleep, his mind slid over scant snatches of dreams from the night before, but he couldn't hold onto them for long. What he did know with concrete certainty was that he was feeling for the first time ever that joy of morning he'd heard in the *Peer Gynt Suite*, and in an odd, half-formed way, it scared him. Because what of that joy's obverse?

Jack was helping Daniel load the paint tins he needed for the day's job in the back of the Holden. Getting a ride with Daniel to the gate, then from there with Juliet and Mel to school, meant he wasn't quite so rushed now in the mornings.

Simon had long since pedalled off.

Jean was leaning against the veranda post, peering through her binoculars at Juliet and Mel's house up on the hill. Jack fervently hoped they weren't looking back down, but somehow he knew they wouldn't be. They wouldn't think to. They were wrapped up cosily in their own lives – not so tightly no one else could get in, but snug enough they were unfazed if others disapproved.

Jean lowered the binoculars and caught Jack's eye.

'So she played records to you all night?' she asked.

'Yes,' said Jack, guarded, sharing a glance with his father as they lifted the last four-litre tin of paint into the back of the station wagon.

Jean slowly put her binoculars back in their leather case.

'Like what?'

Jack pawed at the ground with his foot as Daniel shut the boot.

'Chopin, Debussy, Greg ...'

Jean issued a sharp snort of laughter. '*Greg*?'

Jack blushed. He knew he'd misheard the composer's name.

'Doesn't *she* think she's the cream!'

Daniel shook his head slightly. Jean grimaced. Why couldn't she like Jack more ...? Because she knew he would grow to be Daniel all over again.

'Well, if she's giving you a lift ...' she said, with as much equanimity as she could manage.

Jack began to walk away but stopped and took his bike instead. Something about what his mother had said, her derision of the music they had listened to, had decided him in a plan that he had only toyed with until that moment. Daniel walked over to Jean.

'Jean, if he's made a friend ...'

Daniel reached for her but Jean shrugged and moved away. She stopped suddenly, seeing the household detritus stacked up against the shed, including the old fridge that must have been there ten years, no less!

She couldn't help it. Her frustration welled up.

'Well, we're not going to make any friends with that pile of rubbish still sitting there. How can we have anyone round?'

Jean slammed the door behind her. Daniel surveyed the junk in question. It wasn't junk to him. The fridge was one of the few possessions he had left of his father's, the rest having been pawned to pay off the man's drinking and gambling debts. The fridge was a fifties model, with chrome trimmings and handle. Daniel wanted one day to fix it. Put it in the shed, maybe. One day. One day till one day that day is your last.

He turned, surprised to see Jack had opted for his bike. As Jack disappeared from sight under the arch of trees, Daniel hoped with his whole being that his son would have his day. That day denied most of us.

Jack was at the front gate, watching Juliet and Mel's Citroën come up their parallel driveway and exit their open gate. Pulling up alongside him, both Juliet and Mel gave Jack's bike a questioning glance.

'Gotta go somewhere after school,' he explained cheerfully.

He was just hitching one leg over the seat, when Juliet pressed a button in the car and the boot flew open. Jack knew it would be impolite to refuse. She and Mel called out to see if he needed a hand. He quickly answered that he could manage. He lifted his bike and placed it in as carefully as possible, then found an Ockey strap to keep the boot down. He hopped in the car next to Mel and Juliet drove off.

Juliet was looking fashionable as ever, in a Hawaiian blouse and broomstick skirt. Jack had already heard people saying she put on airs. But maybe she liked to dress up? Maybe she didn't care what others felt. He liked to dress up himself sometimes, as Buck Rogers or Flash Gordon. But he knew you shouldn't dress up in public except when dressing up was the point of the occasion. He then wondered how he knew that.

Mel was wearing some kind of overalls get-up that he'd never seen a girl wear before. She'd get a ribbing at school. But maybe she didn't care either. Next time, he'd wear something odd himself, like a bandanna round his shoulders like he was a cowboy.

Why not!

As they overtook Simon on his bike, Mel wound down the window, leant across Jack and waved. At first Jack tried to stop her but then thought what the hell and stuck his head out with her. The two gawped at Simon vainly trying to keep pace, then spontaneously burst into peals of laughter.

By a strange coincidence, The Kink's 'Autumn Almanac' came on the radio. Jack looked at Mel to discover she was also entranced by it.

Once at school, Jack and Mel got out of the car, and ran off happily to class. It was the first time Jack had ever run to class. Simon arrived on his bike just in time to see them disappearing into their homeroom portable.

He felt a pang of something he'd never felt before, or ever expected to, in relation to his younger brother, but couldn't quite yet name the emotion. All he knew was that it had a garish green hue to it he didn't like at all. Grunting, he chained up his swish red bike next to Jack's bent green one. Even noting the difference in quality couldn't quite eradicate that irksome feeling of ...

Rubbish! He, *jealous* of Jack? But why?

Jack and Mel bounded into class, still laughing and jesting. Abruptly they stopped, trying at once to assume serious expressions. The class was deathly quiet. Up front, Mr Rush, in a wide-collared, tie-dye shirt, was mid-sentence, five rings in five different colours drawn on the blackboard.

'... which is why the Greeks were a very clever lot,' he finished, eying the two speculatively.

The errant pair kept their faces solemn as the class watched them find seats. This time, they sat together at the front.

'Now,' resumed Rush, 'did everyone know that the Greeks started the Olympic Games? Yes? Nowadays, everyone can go. Back then, it was just the men.'

Rush was about to start speaking again when he looked at Jack and Mel. Not for the first time, he noted that they were the only two people of the opposite sex who sat together.

'You know, the rest of you don't have to sit boys down one side, girls down the other. We've come a long way since the Greeks.'

'Miss Jackson made us,' piped up Michael.

Rush smiled. 'You make yourselves.'

Mel's hand shot up.

'Yes, Mel?'

'Why?'

'Why what, young scholar?' asked Rush.

'Why could only the men go to the Olympic Games?'

'Well,' said Rush, 'their society was even more patriarchal than the one we have today.'

Jack noted that Mel didn't even baulk at that strange 'p' word Rush had used – she must have known it!

'Could they at least watch?' she persisted.

'Well, no, my inquisitive friend,' said Rush slowly. 'The men competed naked.'

The class tittered.

'Okay, that's enough,' he responded. 'Now, get out your books. As much as I hate to, I've got notes to dictate.'

The class groaned. They would never have groaned in Higgins' class, and definitely not in Miss Jackson's. Jack watched to see what Rush would do.

Nothing.

In his own way, he seemed every bit as contained, as self-assured – yet not in an arrogant or prideful or defensive fashion – as Juliet and Mel.

Smiling, he simply turned to the blackboard, picked a piece of chalk from the shelf below and began to write, either from memory or making it up as he went, for he wasn't holding notes.

Automatically, Jack snuck out his drawing book, and opened it to a picture he'd started of a crab man. Picking up a black biro, he was about to shade it in when he found his hand hovering over the page. He glanced up at Rush writing on the blackboard, and instead put his lined book on top of his blank one and ruled a margin down the side of the fresh page. From the desk parallel, Michael regarded Jack in astonishment to see him applying himself. Jack shrugged at him good-naturedly.

Mel was keeping good pace with Rush. She had a thick biro containing four nibs you could alternately press down: blue, black, green and red. She kept changing nibs for headings, to make a particular word stand out, or to put in asterisks, and so on.

Jack wanted to laugh. Her page gradually became its own strange, colourful artwork. When the green ink refused to flow, and Mel got annoyed with it, first licking the nib then squiggling on the inside back cover of her book, he nearly laughed. She took notice of him for the first time since class had begun, stared down at her squiggle (actually a colourless indentation) and giggled with him.

They went to their various classes during the day, their last class being with Rush again.

The final school bell rang. The class began to move.

'Uh!' said Rush.

The class sat down again.

'Homework.'

Groaning.

Rush mimicked them. 'It's not that bad! I just want you to do an illustration to the notes we made this morning. Remember, history is something to be valued, so make sure your drawings are factual.'

Glen shot up a hand. 'Can we trace the pictures, Mr Rush?'

Rush adopted the pose and treble of a troll. 'No-o-o!'

There was laughter as Rush walked to the door. He was the only teacher Jack had known who beat his students out the door at home time.

'The Greeks were great artists,' he threw over his shoulder, 'and I expect no less from you lot.'

He reappeared in the doorway a second later.

'No giving up now,' he winked.

Jack stared unblinking as the other students piled out behind him. 'Don't give up' was what Mel had said to him only the night before.

An insistent tugging on his shirt broke the spell. Mel was trying to get him out of his seat, so the two of them could get home as well.

Jack unlocked his bike and they walked to the gate, Mel taking the other handle of the bike like it was a child walking between them. Juliet's Citroën was parked down the street, its engine puttering idly, as the other cars backed away from the curb filled with their cargos of kids.

'Are you going to help me with my drawing, Jack?

He got on his bike. 'No, sorry, Mel, gotta go.'

'Where?'

'Just somewhere,' he threw over his shoulder, copying Rush's gesture and lightness.

She stepped after him as he cycled the opposite direction to home, towards the main drag.

'Somewhere?' Mel shouted.

She stepped after him, unable to mask the petulance in her voice.

'Jack? JACK!'

Her mood changing to thoughtfulness, Mel watched him disappear round a corner before heading over to her mother's car. She could see there was a certain independence in Jack's owning a bike. She made a promise to herself.

The record shop was his father's favourite store in town. It was housed in an old, dim building with bottle green tiles and leadlight windows.

Jack leaned his bike against a green-painted wood seat on the kerb, and walked in cautiously.

The owner was finishing serving a teenage customer, Glen's older brother. Mr Sloane was very pale for country folk, but this was not surprising given his shadowy workplace. He wore a tweed jacket, and had thin, dry hair and a wispy moustache that touched his bottom lip and reminded Jack of Zebedee from *The Magic Roundabout*. Mr Sloane was holding the record on a slant to catch what little coloured light came in from outside.

'*Welcome To My Nightmare*,' Mr Sloane read slowly. His assistant, Anna, who was in her mid twenties, took the record from Mr Sloane, smiled at Glen's brother and put it in a bag for him. Wearing her typical ensemble of skin-tight T-shirt and short skirt, she inspired much discussion among Jack's brother Simon and the older kids.

'Alice Cooper,' mumbled Mr Sloane, looking at the zombie-man on the record cover. 'He doesn't look like an Alice. The things I have to order in.'

Glen's brother hurried out, already pulling the record out of its bag as though he had some way to play it on the street.

Jack walked up to the counter and shyly pulled out the piece of paper he had scribbled on in the Cubby House.

George took the crumpled paper like it might contain something nasty.

'What's this?' he asked, smoothing out its creases and titling his head back so he could peer under his glasses. 'Greg ...? Morning Seat ...? That doesn't make sense.'

Jack felt a surge of anger. 'Morning *Mood*. From the *Peer Gynt Suite*.'

Anna stopped affixing yellow price tags to the latest records, and walked over, gentling taking the slip of paper off Mr Sloane.

'Really, Mr Sloane,' she sighed, her pretty forehead crinkling slightly. 'You know that's Grieg.'

'Yes, that was it!' pounced Jack, then quickly shut his mouth from Mr Sloane's look.

Anna walked to the classical section. 'We should have *that* one,' she said airily.

She had to search right down the back in a little disused pile.

'Like classical music, do you, handsome?'

Jack shuffled on the spot. 'Yes,' he said defensively. 'What's wrong with that?'

Anna laughed pleasantly. 'Nothing!'

She then gave him a funny look. 'So, who do you like?'

Jack eyes searched the walls, as if the answer were there, before nonchalantly answering, 'Oh, Borodin.'

Anna gave him a fetching grin. 'Borodin?'

Jack, still a little tight-lipped and defiant, said shortly, 'Yes.'

'Who else?' she asked encouragingly.

Jack rattled off a list of the composers he'd been introduced to over the past few days.

'Chopin … Debussy … Tchaikovsky …'

Anna sighed with a depth of feeling that, to Jack, seemed out of all proportion, and moved to another stack of records.

'Ah, all the Romantics,' she swooned.

He blushed a deep red. Anna put her hand on his.

'The quality of males round here – why can't you be ten years older?' she winked.

She finally found the record in the first spot she looked, making Jack wonder if she were stalling to have someone else other than Mr Sloane to talk to.

'Ah, knew we had it,' she announced, lifting the record out of the rack.

She walked back to the counter. Following, Jack excavated his pockets.

'How much, please?'

Anna tried to gauge the money he had scrunched up in his hands. 'How much have you got?'

Jack put the notes and coins on the counter. He and Anna counted them.

'Seven dollars and ten cents,' said Jack, dispirited.

Mr Sloane piped in. 'Sorry, young man, those records are – '

Anna cut him off. 'Half price, aren't they, Mr Sloane?'

Mr Sloane grunted.

'Thought so,' said Anna, slipping the record into a paper bag. 'Well, my young Romantic, it's yours.'

Smiling, Jack pushed his way through the door, the bell still chiming long after it banged shut. Mr Sloane walked over to Anna at the till.

'Young Miss, are we running a business or a charity?'

Anna gave him a severe glance. 'A service, Mr Sloane.'

'Well, do me a service and make up the difference.'

Mr Sloane returned self-importantly to his present task as Anna reached with inexplicable weariness, for one so young, into her purse.

Jack threw open the front door. Jean, Daniel and Simon looked up from the dinner table.

'Where have you been?' asked Jean. 'Do you know what time it is?'

'Just out, Mum,' said Jack, heading to his room to dispense with his prize cargo.

'Your dinner's cold,' she called after him.

Jack emerged from his room, snatched up plate and utensils, and headed to the front door.

'Where are you off to now?' she asked.

'Homework. I'll do it in the shed.'

'You, doing homework?' Daniel asked, jokingly.

As Jack kicked the front door shut behind him, he just had time to hear Jean ask Simon, 'What's this new teacher like?' and Simon's response: 'Dunno, Smithy says he's a bit of a ...'

Jack was sitting at Daniel's red work desk with its white drawers and red handles, wrapt in his task, his coloured pencils fanned out before him, and a blank piece of paper beneath his hands which he rapidly filled with a vibrant, whirling vision. Beside him, sat the books he'd borrowed from the school library, their pages laid open to pictures of Greek Attic Vases, marble statues, ancient stone friezes and contemporary renditions of their sport and war; all the source material to make his picture as vivid and bold as time and inexperience allowed.

It was a new direction for Jack; still fantastical in bent, but wonderment allied to reality and research.

He'd never before been so engaged by a school assignment. It was as if it directly called on his skills. Not even art class engaged him, where he was forced along with the other kids to adhere to set projects. Just today, they had been made to halve potatoes, dip the resulting flat faces in white paint, and stamp these on large sheets of yellow cardboard to make oddly oval clouds. He was then compelled along with them to empty clag glue along the bottom of the paper and then pour sand on this to represent the beach. The sort of technique that Jack had mastered, under his father's watchful eye, at the age of four. Oh, and the odd way the other kids would draw a rectangle of blue along the tops of their pages even though they'd drawn ground way below. As if the sky stopped in the clouds!

Oddly, Daniel never drew himself; he only offered guidance. 'It hurts,' was his excuse. Jack did not know Daniel to have anything wrong with his hands and wondered if he was pained in a more obscure, abstract fashion.

The only interruption to Jack's progress on the picture came each time he got up to put the needle back to the beginning of 'Powerman' by the Kinks. The song had just the right kind of throbbing intensity necessary to get the assignment finished. If only record players had a button where you could loop certain tracks.

So absorbed was he in his task, he didn't know Jean was leaning over his shoulder, the expression on her face acquiring the sickly glean of shock.

'Jack!'

Jack literally started from his seat. 'What?' he quavered, now standing.

Jean thrust a finger at the drawing. 'What's this … *filth*?'

Her finger hovered over the exposed genitals of the naked charioteer.

'It's homework, Mum.'

Jean's expression tautened.

'Homework? Naked men ...? You'd better explain yourself, boy.'

Jack peered up at his mother timidly, wondering what he'd done wrong.

Chapter 9

In the living room, Daniel had to lean back to focus on the drawing, Jean held it so close to his face. She'd ripped it angrily from Jack's exercise book.

'Getting kids to draw this filth! Wait till I tell Marcia Jackson what kind of person is filling in for her.'

Daniel put down the boots he'd been polishing and peeked over the book at Jack, who was standing in his bedroom doorway.

'Jack! Have you re-drawn it yet?' asked Jean.

Jack nodded in the affirmative.

Jean clicked her fingers. 'Let's see it.'

Jack entered the room and showed her the new picture. This time, the charioteer's genitals were concealed by the front of the chariot.

Jean scrutinized it a long moment before holding it before Daniel's eyes a second and snapping the book shut.

'Better. I think I'll talk to Mr Higgins tomorrow.'

'Oh, Jean, surely ...' Daniel started, but Jean spoke over him.

'*Tomorrow*.' She turned to Jack. 'Now go to bed.'

Jack stretched out his arm. Jean handed over his exercise book and Jack slipped through his door and shut it solemnly behind him.

Daniel had only seen a glimpse of the redrawn picture but he was impressed. His son had clearly inherited what little talent he had, but what sort of gift was it if it brought wrath, guilt and joylessness? He hoped Jack would be one of the special few who reaped the rewards of their abilities in their own lifetimes …

Probably not.

The magpies were particularly noisy as Jack woke. But he loved all the morning calls the birds made. Mornings could be wondrous things, he decided, because the day can still be anything you want it to be. Late afternoons, it's as set as the sun, as curtained as the world is at that revolution of the celestial clock.

When he got to the breakfast table, Daniel had already left for work – lately, he could only get jobs in the next town, fifty kilometres away. Simon was on the shag rug, doing his exercises.

'Your friend rang,' said Jean tersely. 'They can't give you a lift.'

Jack wondered what might be the matter as he rode his bike up the yellow road, the grass edging it just as yellow. Payback from Mel for not riding home with her yesterday? It didn't seem her style. When he got to the gate, he was surprised to see Mel on a bike of her own; a glittering gold contraption with a banana seat.

She had the fence open for him so he had only to ride through and shut it. He felt silly and mean for thinking it was any reason but a logical and fun one.

Higgins had got to school early, and was sitting in his office, trying to get on top of his paperwork before the teachers and students marred the stillness of the place with their noise and activity.

He had almost finished adjusting the ins and outs register when Jean rang. He began the usual pleasantries but his voice soon petered out and he listened in silence. The implications of what she said threatened to dredge up an old incident in his own past he thought he'd successfully put out of his mind.

'Yes, thank you, Mrs. Bennett,' he muttered grimly. 'I'll look into it.'

Putting the phone down in its cradle, he turned to look out his casement window just as the dapper Rush strolled into view. What timing! Oblivious to the corollary in Higgins' mind, Rush waved.

A big, clumsy man, with a shambling step, Higgins pressed his face to the glass in Rush's classroom door as unobtrusively as he could. The glass reminded Higgins of the viewing portals he'd seen on TV in the doors to prison cells. Yes, they had their uses. Both examples.

He observed Rush stroll around the class, looking at the kids' pictures of the ancient Olympics.

'Good … Well done … Nice colouring.'

Rush stopped short at Jack's desk and scrutinised the boy's drawing with growing astonishment. He knew Jack had talent from the other day but this … He tried to make himself give Mel, sitting next to Jack, an encouraging smile, but while she evidently had preternatural gifts in nearly all subjects, drawing was the exception. Mel's sardonic expression seemed to indicate she knew as much herself, and she gazed at Jack's picture, thereby giving Rush the implicit freedom to solely focus on it too.

'Oh my, Jack, that's very good,' he said at last.

The line, the colouring, perspective, composition …

'All excellent,' he declared. 'Although ... the legs are a little short!'

Jack huffed. They'd been the right proportion in his first rendition. The charioteer's groin was now beneath the front of the chariot but it did make him appear an amputee below the knees.

'Yes, well …' he mumbled.

Laughing, Rush put a hand on Jack's shoulder.

Higgins, watching and straining his ears behind the glass in the door, stiffened at the sight of Rush's touch.

'Never mind. Perhaps he's kneeling,' quipped Rush.

Rush turned and strolled to the other half of the class where all the girls sat except Mel. He stopped at Emma and Kate's desk. They had each drawn rather crude pictures of discus throwers with enormous penises.

Rush rubbed his chin. 'Hmm. Nice work, girls, but you need to learn a thing or two about proportion ...'

Emma and Kate giggled as Rush surveyed the remainder of the other girls' work. He was relieved none of them had attempted to draw their figures naked. Perhaps it had been unwise to introduce the concept to their heads. Well, Mel had asked why only the men could attend the ancient Olympics and he wasn't about to lie to a kid.

He hoped soon to answer that other question Mel didn't yet know to ask.

Tomorrow evening they were going to tell her. Together. He and Juliet.

It was afternoon and Rush's class was lying on the floor of the music room, in Higgins' care. Higgins evaluated them, feeling put out. The usual teacher who took them for Music had called in sick again, the neurotic thing. Getting the kids to lie down with eyes closed was evidently how she began proceedings. Higgins spied the record player and walked over to it.

He cleared his voice; always a good idea to air the throat, even if only to address children.

'Now, Mr Rush has been telling you that music can help you travel to places,' he intoned, then pinned one of the students with his grey eyes. 'Is that so, Kate?'

Kate's eyes flicked open. 'Yes, Mr Higgins!'

Higgins screwed up his face.

'Hmm ... Well, in fact, music is a very precise science. Mathematics, if you will. Classical music makes one smarter.'

Having felt that with these few words he righted a dangerous misconception brewing in these impressionable minds, while at the same time not appearing to contradict another teacher, he turned and sorted through the small stack of records beside the piano, as he muttered half to himself.

'Any Brahms? I find Brahms eminently sensible. Never mind, it will have to be Tchaikovsky. Somewhat overwrought, but ...'

Higgins placed the needle down on the spinning record. 'Tchaikovsky's *Piano Concerto No. 1*,' he announced.

Jack, who until then had been silently busy trying to name just what it was he was looking at with eyes closed – strange, continent-long, crustaceans in space was all he could manage; the infusoria of old imaginings – forgot these creatures in an instant and became immediately entranced with the opening, blazing few bars. Bleating horns, swooning strings, ascending piano chords and a theme immediately melodic, immediately arresting, frenetic but still somehow ... that word his father introduced to him sprang to mind ... melancholic.

Yes, whatever this sound was, it was deeply sad. He opened his eyes. Embarrassingly, he realised Mel was looking at his no doubt screwed-up face. It wasn't an 'I caught you out look', though, but that one of understanding he had so quickly come to expect, to rely on for buoyancy. How had he ever coped with never being understood before? (Except by Daniel, perhaps.) She started moving her mouth like a fish in time with the music, and Jack could do nothing but laugh, his melancholy evaporating in an instant.

Higgins pulled the needle off the record, enacting a sudden violence on that magic.

'Mel!' he boomed.

Mel sat up and, with an innocent air and sugary voice, asked, 'Yes, Mr Higgins?

Higgins exploded at the impudence. To not even pretend to feel shame for being caught out. Instead, to sarcastically mock him. A child!

'You might think we're in the sticks here, young girl, but courtesy is still important. I'll see you in my office tomorrow morning.'

Jack sat up with Mel. Their classmates remained lying down, as if held there by the force of Higgins' censure.

'But, Mr Higgins,' Mel pronounced, 'tomorrow's Saturday.'

Higgins' raised eyebrows momentarily truncated the expanse of his forehead as his mind tabulated this fact. Tomorrow was indeed Saturday, but he couldn't back down in front of an eleven-year-old girl.

'Well, er, yes … exactly! Tomorrow's Saturday – ha!'

Mel turned her swan-like neck with the choreography of a ballerina and fixed her eyes on Jack, both only managing not to laugh through biting their lips.

When Jack got home, he noticed something moving by the water trough. Jumping the fence, he found a sheep on its own, lying on the ground, panting. He looked down the valley to see his Dad pulling up in the station wagon.

The sheep's eyes were sticking out. Grimly, Daniel leant down and parted its wool to find hundreds of wriggling maggots.

'I told John they needed shearing again,' he cursed.

He immediately set off for John Harrow's property, Jack tailing after him.

John turned off his tractor engine and led them inside his house, asking Daniel why he didn't just keep a gun himself. At the mention of guns, Jack winced, knowing what that meant.

'I don't find them congenial company,' grumbled Daniel.

At that, John's expression hardened. He took them to his living room where his daughter Emma and her friend Kate were playing with makeup. They looked at Jack and made faces. John got on a stool and took down the rifle hanging over the fireplace.

He showed them outside via a different route, going through his rumpus room where there was a wall of medals and photos of John in military garb.

Taking two bullets from a box, John handed them to Daniel. Before he let go, he pinned Daniel with his stare. 'I, for one, am not ashamed of what we did over there.'

Daniel would not explain to Jack what that meant. He was keen to get back and put the sheep out of its misery. Once home, he told Jack to go inside and, quaking in his limbs, turned in the direction of the sheep. As Jack hurried away, he heard his father mutter, 'I don't get this world ... I'll never get it.'

The poor sheep, thought Jack. The troubling notion occurred to him that it wasn't just humans who could be cruel, with their stupid Saturday detentions and things. The whole world could, from nature up, be far more malevolent.

He worried he would never understand life either.

That night, in the shed, with Daniel sharpening the blades on the lawn mower and Jack drawing, he asked his father which was his favourite Kinks song.

'Days', said Daniel unhesitatingly.

Jack found the song on one of Daniel's records and listened to it.

Thank you for the days,
Those endless days, those sacred days you gave me

It was sport tomorrow afternoon. Jack was never good at sport but he and Daniel would be expected by Jean to attend Simon's game. Yet there was only one place Jack wanted to be tomorrow, even if it was a locale he usually despised, and would never normally think about attending on a weekend.

He tuned back into the song and wondered if in time it might become his favourite Kinks masterpiece, too.

Days I'll remember all my life,
Days when you can't see wrong from right

But then that equivocation which seemed always to come with a Kinks song:

But then I knew that very soon you'd leave me

Jack balled up his fist, and pounded his knee with it, his father giving him a funny look. No, that part was wrong. If they were sacred days, *endless* days, how could they cease? Jack sensed his first disagreement brewing with his father: the Kinks weren't flawless after all.

The morning sun burnished the grounds of Miller's Creek School with a blazing copper.

Higgins responsibly arrived at the detention he'd set Mel a good twenty minutes early, and then sat in doleful silence. Why so conscientious on his part? She would turn up either on the dot or late. A horrid feeling came over him that had reared itself of late like another voice inside him. Or an old voice he thought he'd forgotten: his dead, younger self. It had the one, pressing question: is this the best of life, teaching children punctuality?

Half an hour later, he looked up from his desk to see that Mel had moved to her usual seat at the back of the empty class and was busily moving her hands. He watched as she weaved a cat's cradle between her fingers from red wool.

Exasperated, he was about to ask her to come to the front of class, and to continue with the assignment he'd given her, when he noticed it was sitting in front of him: a full page's worth, in her inimitably sensible script.

Picking up the paper, he began reading with little doubt his chosen topic of 'Paying Respect to Teachers' had been subverted.

He'd only scanned the first preposterous but disturbingly brilliant sentence when he heard footsteps and a creaking sound. He turned to the opened door.

'Jack!' Mel cried.

Higgins flicked his gaze to her. She'd called Jack's name in a way no one had ever called his.

'Mr Higgins, I ...' Jack stumbled.

The boy had, on his part, looked at Mel in a way Higgins had, likewise, never looked at another. Certainly, in a way no one had ever looked at *him*.

'Jack, it's not necessary,' Higgins said quickly, wanting, perversely, to sever their connection. 'Run along.'

Jack remained in the doorway, defiant. Higgins examined the boy, and felt oddly beyond his depth.

Jack held up his chin. 'I did it too, Mr Higgins.'

That voice of youth in Higgins called out. Stifling it, he pushed Mel's essay away. He knew he'd never get back to it now.

He softened his tone. 'Well, at least you're man enough to say so. Now go on, Jack.'

When Jack again did not budge, Higgins made a shooing motion with his hand, and felt a stab of absurdity.

Jack's next word made the feeling more acute.

'No.'

'No?' queried Higgins, feeling his quiet anger returning; the one emotion he could rely on to sustain him.

'No,' said Jack, with all the authority one should ever need. 'I'm staying.'

What a gulf of years there was separating them, thought Higgins, as he stared at Jack and Jack at he. And yet it had once been *he*, Higgins, standing on the other side of that age divide, in front of a teacher he had no doubt thought ridiculous in his ignorance. His hand flew to his forehead, swabbing his damp brow with a taupe handkerchief.

No, he'd never been a Jack. Or a Mel either, for that matter.

'Very well,' he said, cornered. 'You can join your accomplice.'

Jack felt a sense of pride no homework assignment had given him. Until Rush's, that is, before it had been soured.

No, thought Higgins, reading the triumph in the boy's face. Damn him, a mere child, for making a fifty-five-year-old feel small!

Higgins adopted a tone of profound displeasure. 'Your mother will be very disappointed in you, Jack.'

Jack sat down, the light going out in him, but Mel smiled in such a matter-of-fact way, as if none of this mattered in the least, that it was immediately reignited.

Daniel was home alone. For the first time in his adult life, he was worried about being alone. But at least it was better than being in company. Because he never knew when 'it' might happen. 'It' was his growing panic that if ever anyone showed him any sympathy, he might break down and cry.

The prospect of crying when he thought he had left behind tears along with other childish things, especially in front of an audience, was of a magnitude of horror he could not even bear contemplating.

Don't show me any kindness. Don't anyone ever show me any... and, most likely to completely floor me ... sympathy, had become his desperate prayer.

Yes, better he was alone. Jean was in town with Simon, getting new studs for his boots before the big off-season game, and Jack had gone off on a long bike ride. He hadn't said where to; he hadn't needed to. Daniel knew he should accomplish some task before they all got home and they went to the match. He looked at Jean's long-standing 'To do' list pinned to the fridge before heading to the shed and grabbing tools appropriate to the task he'd chosen. As he stepped on a paint tin to reach up to a high sill to collect his tape measure, his eye caught a blanket hanging in the furthest recess of the shed. He tried to get back to the task ahead, but hopped down, and walked over to the blanket and pulled it away instead.

All his long-forgotten, half-finished canvasses stood before him, slightly resentful. Flicking through them like he might flick through an oversized stack of records, he found the one above all others he had to look at just now.

Wiping the surface gently with a clean, damp rag, he rested it on his workbench and stood back. It depicted a boy and a girl, standing several metres apart beside a pond in a walled garden, watching each other with infinite patience and understanding and ... care.

It was of him and Juliet at Jack and Mel's ages now. He'd painted them in the suit and dress they'd worn to Juliet's mother's funeral.

He noted his painter's box with used oil brushes in it. Picking one out, he flicked the bristles through his fingers thoughtfully. But should he revisit a scene of the past? *Could* he?

And besides, the painting was finished.

He nearly jumped when Jean walked past the open door carrying a load of washing.

'Daniel, that rubbish won't move by itself. You've still got time.'

How had he not heard her and Simon pulling up in the turning circle? He put down the brush, picking up a pair of work gloves instead. He knew the job she had in mind for him and it wasn't the one he had chosen.

Chapter 10

Juliet sat at her bay window, which was marvellously closed in with sheltering trees. A cup of camomile tea warmed her hands, its aroma wringing the air. She sighed. To have her daughter taken from her for even a morning, with such a stupid reason as a detention, was utterly ridiculous. Juliet had gone for as long a walk as she could manage that morning, to the end of their dirt road where it intersected with the bitumen one, and had peeked through the poplars forming something of a windbreak between properties. She saw Jack closing his gate, jumping back on his bike, and pedalling off. She knew suddenly, instinctively, just where he was headed and felt afresh the pang of nostalgia for the friendship she and his father had shared many years before. Joining Mel in her ignominy was just the sort of thing Daniel would have done for her, too.

Juliet trembled as she took from a paper-lined drawer the only photo she had of her and Daniel as kids, holding it in the curtain-diffused light from the window, tracing a figure-eight around them with her fingers, a clean circle track amid the dust. What an odd time it had been, the two of them dressed for a funeral, which led to that fateful choice. To stay with her aunt, who lived with them, or to join her father overseas in Europe. Her decision to go had led to her brilliant career and the best thing that had come into her life.

Tonight, Dash would come, and tonight she would begin to let go of Mel. Had to.

'Too soon, too soon!' she cried. 'Too soon.'

Would Dash stay on in Miller's Creek? A man of the arts: of the world? The parallels, the repetition of history – the strange, maddening circle.

She lifted herself off the divan and stumbled against the mantelpiece, knocking one of the items she'd brought with her to the floor. Dizzily, she retrieved and unfolded the Japanese fan, a prop she'd been allowed to keep from one of her operatic triumphs, and a favourite item.

She went to her record cabinet and found the album the fan suggested to her. Skipping the needle to the aria she liked best, she began to sing.

Mel looked up from her doodles of fans and dresses to stare straight at Higgins. Higgins looked back vaguely, then gazed out the window. Although three kilometres away, somehow he too could hear the aria. Higgins appeared to be mesmerized by the music.

'All right, you can go,' he said.

Jack was puzzled at the strange look on Higgins' face, but then he, too, heard it. Or *did* he hear it? Was it in his and Mel's heads and were they were imparting some of it to Higgins in a bleeding transmission? It was worthy of a scene from *Doctor Who*.

With infinite slowness, Mel got up from her desk and walked out the door. Jack followed.

They stepped into the corridor where Mel bade Jack stop and look.

'At what?' he asked.

'Look again.'

Vines were growing on the drab corridor walls. He and Mel rushed down it, the plaster turning to stone before their eyes.

The next thing they knew, they were in that garden in the roofless ruin behind Mel and Juliet's house. But this time, all the decay and overgrowth had been tenderly cleared away, revealing a pond with a scalloped stone fountain.

Jack found himself wearing a suit and Mel was in the first dress he'd seen her in, a lovely, white flowing thing.

Daniel looked at the old fifties fridge with its antique yellow finish, chrome art deco flourishes, and sighed. He wanted to keep it and fix it up, but he knew it was just as easy to take it to the tip. The rest of the rubbish pile that Jean found so offensive he could dispose of more easily on their property. He backed his Holden up to the fridge, opened the boot and reached in for ropes, wondering how he would lift it in on his own.

Brute strength?

He consulted his watch. Jack should be back by now, with Simon's game scheduled for the afternoon.

Daniel crouched down, lifting underneath the fridge, when he heard an unfamiliar sound intermingling with his groaning.

Lowering the fridge back to the ground he turned to spy Juliet's property at the top of the hill. Jean always complained about how isolated they were, nestled in the valley, but occasionally the wind could do that, pick up a noise, a half-song of birds, the bleating of a sheep, and sweep it down to them. But not for a long time had they heard human sounds.

The fridge forgotten, he walked slowly to the stile bridging the two properties, the beautiful transcendent singing falling like a light rain after a decades-long summer.

Mel stood up from the water's edge where she had been kneeling and stepped before Jack. Each stood perfectly still, looking into the other's eyes across the distance of an arm's length.

'You've found me,' said Mel happily.

For some unaccountable reason, Jack felt himself on the precipice of tears.

'I ...' he choked.

Smiling, Mel held a finger to his lips.

'Shhh.'

As Daniel stepped over the stile, he could better make out Juliet's exquisite tones dancing upon a song he'd only heard on the radio, but knew to be from the opera *The Mikado*. Juliet's clear voice conjured a world of experience, of magic created and sustained, if only for a night's entertainment, a night's relief from the shabbiness of everyday life. The beauty, the tenderness of that voice! A grief staked his heart. What things he hadn't seen! What places, what lives, art, music, theatre. What worlds upon worlds.

His one venture overseas had been to a well of senseless depravity and horror. Yet there was a duality to life, a beauty that made the darkness all the more unnecessary ... heartbreaking.

What beauty he had never sought, never tripped wonderingly in search of, tried to catch in hide and seek.

The sun, whose rays are all ablaze
With ever-living glory ...

The light, the glory, the effulgence. There were artists who transmuted the broiling fears and hopes of the soul, and what had he done?

'I mean to rule the earth as he the sky ...' she sang, '... the sun and I ...'

He paused, the waving grass a false audience. Were those words for him? He punched his knee. How vain of him, how falsely inflated to think he mattered. What had he to offer to one who'd gone out in the world, one who 'lights up well'? That he, Daniel, should not have mattered to her, that she left him, he could only echo the aria: 'I, for one, don't blame her!'

He paused again, closeted amid the ghost gums. And yet ... the mutual insomnia, the light in her house that he had seen from his, that light he'd seen at one, two, three in the morning as he wrestled himself from Jean's ever more fearful grip, and made his way to the dining room window ...

We're very wide awake,
The moon and I

Could she have been, from her window, reaching out her heart and mind to him as tremulously, fatefully?

Rubbish! He was a failure. Nothing. How could he matter to someone who 'means to rule the earth ...' and did. *Had*. In her exceptional career.

But did she rule 'as he the sky'?

She knows her worth, but no, not I.

No. He wasn't the sun to her moon. Daniel accepted what he had known for a long time but never before dared articulate, for fear the already fragile tissue of his life would rip to confetti. He counted for nothing, and never had.

Mel gestured for Jack to follow. They pushed through a hedge to see a stream. A black swan was swimming along the inky, giddying swirls with its chicks. Mel watched them and laughed. Then, in a flash, she turned to Jack, a furious expression on her brow he'd never before seen. A revulsion, a distaste for … no, not life … but everything that is its antithesis.

'The world could be so good,' she hissed.

Jack scoped from Mel to the swans in their perfect serenity. He knew there were two meanings to good. Good as in great and good as in …

Mel parted another hedge. On the other side was Juliet in her lounge room, singing that beautiful song. But it was in the real world and Jack wanted to stay in the magical garden forever.

Mel pushed her way through the hedge.

'No, Mel, not yet!'

She walked up to her mum, while he held back. Suddenly, as if gripped in pain, Juliet fell to the floor, clutching her head.

Mel's cry shattered the air. 'Mum! Are you all right?'

Jack rushed forward, leaving their briefly forged realm of dream.

'Yes. Yes, I'm okay, dear.'

With difficulty, Jack and Mel helped her to her feet. Juliet extricated herself from their caring hands and brightened up. Daniel appeared shyly at the open French windows. He watched for a few seconds before Jack noticed him.

'Dad!'

'Sorry, heard your singing ... Beautiful. Except perhaps that last note.'

Mel blushed.

Daniel caught Jack's eye. 'Um, Jack, just wanted to remind you we need to be getting to Simon's game.' He immediately felt morose with the words he'd just uttered, their sheer, offensive banality. He might as well have mentioned the pleasantness of the cool breeze.

He and Juliet shared a long look, Daniel feeling like a fuddy duddy. The children examined their respective parents questioningly, then Jack tugged on Daniel's hand.

'Come on, Dad.'

Mel followed. 'I'm going too, Mum.'

'Mel! If it's all right with Dan?'

Huffily, Mel drew her arms across her chest. Daniel smiled consent, and Mel and Jack raced off ahead of him, down the hill. Daniel shrugged at Juliet as though to say he had no choice but to follow. He started to back away through the open door but stopped. If nothing else, he would at least stand above the pettiness, the jealousies, of his fellow townsfolk, and acknowledge Juliet's success. For he was proud of her: genuinely and without rancour.

He looked her straight in the eye. 'I owe you congratulations, Juliet.'

She examined him quizzically.

'You never gave up.'

In that one expression Juliet could intuit a whole world of disappointment in Daniel, an understanding his incipient talents had never been acknowledged, tutored and brought to prominence as they had been in her.

What might she have done for him, if she'd only thought to try? Always accounted a success, what was she in this respect? Where might *she* be now, if it weren't for her mother's chance meeting with her worldly father, a man from Europe she'd met in town, and his considerable contacts on the continent? If Juliet had stayed, she might have *him*, Daniel, but would that embrace have been enough to cancel out the other disappointment, a thwarted career? For every win, a loss. For each choice made, a million denied.

Life is lonely.

Daniel turned and followed after Jack and Mel, who were already quite a way down the hill.

Juliet held her hand to her breast. 'You never gave up,' he had said to her. No. She had given up in one aspect of her life. She'd given up on him! And when she'd finally come back to the place and person she could never forget, it was too late. Far too late.

For she was dead.

Or soon would be.

Simon was playing a home game against the visiting football team, from nearby Hahndorf, the spectators on the sideline cheering them on, Jean the loudest. Whenever Jean nudged him, Daniel yelled too, but far less vociferously. Simon kicked a goal. Jean and half the sideline roared. Jack looked at his brother lapping up the acclaim and then at his approving mother. Mel nudged him and smiled. Jack couldn't help but smile back. She took his hand.

'Come.'

The two snuck off, only Daniel noticing. But he said nothing. These days of youthful optimism would be over for them before long. He would not begrudge them a single hour, nay, minute.

That evening, when Jack and Mel returned to Juliet's, Mel confirmed Jack's very chivalrous appearance at her detention that morning, and related how he'd refused to leave.

Feeling her heart aflutter, Juliet told Mel to chaperone Jack to the stile and to come back quickly, since they had a guest arriving soon. When they left, she feverishly rang Jack's house, hoping Daniel would answer.

'Juliet?' he asked.

'Daniel, I've sent Jack down. But … I really rang to say … I mean, I want to congratulate *you* on your great achievement.'

Daniel grabbed the doorjamb with violence. What had he to be congratulated on? What torture, this? And from Juliet?

Juliet turned to look out the window, to see rollicking with her girl the just as incomparable …

'Jack,' she whispered.

Daniel quickly rung off, worried he would blubber like a child.

Walking up the hill to meet Jack, Daniel tracked the progress of a purple Valiant travelling along the ridge to Juliet's place. He knew from the gossips whose car it was. Well, what was he thinking anyway? From what Jack had told him, Rush was well-travelled, sophisticated, erudite …

A small, fragile edifice of potential happiness he'd built within his soul on Juliet's return, caved in on itself with the sight of Rush alighting at Juliet's porch, and her greeting him with a fervent embrace. The dust of hope whirled in one final eddy before settling upon him as the shadow that hitherto had lengthened across his whole life. Only this time it was made darker, for the brief contrast of light her presence and Mel's had brought.

He looked up at the marvellously blue sky; as if this part of the world had just been dunked under delicious water, all the colours running to a turquoise, muddy brown.

He loved the land but was ambivalent about the people. Yet there was no one to blame but himself for staying put.

He knew he would ball if anyone showed him any sympathy. He hoped to hell people went on not noticing him. At least Jack and Mel were happy, and he wanted to do anything in his means to keep them in that state.

Chapter 11

The next couple of weeks were a joy all round. Rush's presence had taken out a choice in Daniel's life that probably wasn't there to begin with. It angered him somewhat he was relieved from making a decision, but then he had responsibilities and so it wasn't really his decision to make. And while Jean went on about the impropriety of a mother having a dalliance with her daughter's teacher, it was obvious she felt relief too.

Daniel enjoyed tête-à-têtes with Juliet, although brief, as each took it in turns to host the other's kid, for Jack was either at Mel's place, or Mel was at their place, but rarely the two apart.

He enjoyed that these exchanges were not chaperoned by Jean, her sense of danger having all but passed. He appreciated this 'freedom' despite the implicit slight to his character. Was he really so 'safe' after all?

Yes, probably.

But was he being honourable? Or merely honourable by default? And what arrogance on his own part to think his feelings were in any small way reciprocated.

Jean warmed slightly to Mel, but nonetheless worried she was dragging Jack away from more manly pursuits in which his older brother engaged, and which he was normally inclined to avoid anyway. She didn't have much truck with all this listening to music, or gazing in art books, or making costumes, choreographing dances, composing songs, constructing pictures, putting on shows; in short, all the stuff of indoor activity in the height of summer.

It wasn't as if Mel, or Jack for that matter, was entirely averse to outdoor engagement. In truth, much the opposite, with all their tree climbing, bike riding, nocturnal walks between each other's properties. It's just that it all involved an imaginative, fantastical component which bothered Jean, but in which Daniel could find no fault. Of course, Juliet did not even seem to notice, it felt so natural to her; the infinite rubric of make-believe.

Jack and Mel became wonderfully helpful to Daniel, with shifting the sheep from one paddock to the next, gathering up firewood, collecting the eggs from the hens, and all the other farmyard duties. Mel especially became quite an excellent little drover in their musters. She asked why they didn't have dogs to assist and Jack showed her the two stone mounds behind the settler's huts in remembrance of their kelpies. Telling her the story, she promised never to move them.

This all went well till Jean began to involve Simon in her domestic chores and activities, something from which she'd previously exempted him given his all-important dream of becoming a state footballer. The outcome was to make Simon resent, not Jean, but Jack and Mel all the more. Daniel wished Jean would not respond that way and tried to encourage Jack and Mel to help her, but when they would run between the clotheslines, pressing their faces against the sheets to mimic ghosts, and whatever other tomfoolery they put their genius for joy into, she would get so unaccountably exasperated. It wasn't as if they didn't do the work; they just elevated it to a game. And this was life, her life now, and she saw they were making fun of it. Rather than making *it* fun.

The suns, whose rays are all ablaze ...

They really knew their worth, the sun and her.

For Jack's part, he got to know Rush better too. His full name was Dashiell Landon Rush, 'Dash' for short. There was some fun about the middle name thing when it was discovered Jack did not possess one. He was simply Jack Bennett. Mel was in fact Mallika Evangeline Jeffries, and Juliet was Juliet Poppy Jeffries.

Rush behaved much as he did at school. Which would have been dreadful if he'd been any of the other teachers. But he was friendly, cordial to kid and adult alike. Only, Jack noted a strangeness between him and Juliet, a secret shared. When he could, Dash would drive her all the way to the doctors in Adelaide for 'routine' tests.

The two would sit on the porch and say nothing for hours at a time, or laugh and joke uproariously. Once, Jack saw Juliet sobbing into Dash's arms when he'd run back to the house alone from the Cubby House to collect more paper for their drawings – Mel was too busily engaged in gluing to suffer an interruption – when Jack chanced on the, to him, inexplicable scene. They had neither seen him and nor did he tell Mel out of a tacit understanding with himself that he should never speak wherefore he did not fully comprehend.

On Daniel's part, he first met Dash at the stile. Dash was riding the rather bored mare from the neighbour's property beyond Juliet's at breakneck speed up and down the paddock.

'Hope you don't mind,' he said, reigning the mare in to a splash of sods. 'Did an awful lot of polo one time. A snob's game for the most part, but the only way to get noticed in the rarefied circles I asphyxiated in. Dash.'

Daniel reached up and took his hand.

Daniel had never expected to meet Rush and had not prepared an attitude with which to confront the reality. He rather felt he should have hated the man but instead found him instantly likeable and quite genial, and he took a great interest in Daniel's scheme for pumping water from the creek to the concrete troughs in the paddocks not fronting the water. And how Daniel had worked out schemes of natural downhill pressure for the excess to run off into their somewhat haphazardly planted and thought-out garden. It was a level of interest no one could have maintained without it proceeding from a genuine core, and so their in-depth conversation on pipe diameters, faucets, pump engines and other farming matters was one of the most unexpected afternoons of his life.

He felt afterwards something he'd been unable to place before, and that was an acute sense of not having anyone with whom to share these banal intimacies. He and Jean 'lived together' in only the most superficial sense of that phrase.

They met only two more times, and again enjoyed cordial exchanges on both occasions. Daniel admitted to himself that Rush was a massively attractive individual. For some reason, women could say that out loud about other women but men could not say the same about other men, because it brought out ugly words. Daniel felt he had little to be proud of, but he was honest enough to admit Rush was the sort of person he wished he could have been, or at the very least properly befriend.

Because he was lonely. He was infinitely lonely. There wasn't a single bloke in town he could properly call a mate. His son was his best friend.

And the love of his life, the woman with whom this Rush was spending so much time, was both within physical reach and never further from his arms.

Besides, he had his family.

Like many a miserable married couple, he and Jean were putting their energies into their children. Yet not even in this were they united. They had chosen one each.

Jean *did* drag Jack to the pool one Saturday with her and Simon, insisting Daniel stay at home. It would be just her, her two boys and she even condescended to include Mel.

The concrete surrounding the pool burnt the soles of their feet. Jack and Mel made their way to the shallow end. Jack normally took forever to get in – if he wasn't 'encouraged' with a push, that is – but this time he jumped straight in of his own accord. The gasp exploded up his body, and he splashed furiously to get warm. Even in summer the pool was always cold. Mel got in the way he normally did – by increments – making a great deal of fuss in the process.

They stayed in the shallows since the big kids, including Simon and Troy, the friend he always seemed to hang off, were bombing in the deep end. The year before, the postman's son had drowned that way. He had jumped in but was unable to return to the surface with all the other kids unthinkingly bombing on top of him. They weren't meant to bomb anymore, but for some reason no one stopped them.

When Jack and Mel got out, they walked freely on the hot concrete this time, their wet soles affording their protection. They bought a Redskin each for twenty cents from the canteen then Mel followed Jack's example and found a bare stretch of ground to lie on. There they lay a good while, in a wet outline of their own bodies, two dead kids who hadn't yet been removed from the scene of the crime. Arms folded in front, they eyed each other, blinking in the reflected glare from the sun on the blinding concrete.

Slowly, as they dried, the ground would become intolerably hot again. And so another quick dip, and then another, until the lengthening shadows of the trees made even the concrete cool. By which time, they would no doubt complain of sore backs, necks and shoulders from the sun, and peel for the next few days.

Jean had spent a pleasant afternoon tanning and chatting with the other mothers about all the local scandals. Simon didn't bother them but Jack did notice his brother splashing a girl by the slide and trying to get her to laugh with him. When they left, she didn't even look at Simon. But Simon was looking at Jack with Mel hard enough. He was searching for something in them, like there was a secret to their bond he would never unlock.

Simon turned away from them. But he could not so easily turn from his sense of gnawing dread. For whatever was the cause of his failure, it was welling from within.

On one of the dusky, purple eves, Mel and Jack were with Daniel in the shed, where Daniel had renewed his fervour for handyman activities. Mel got up to put on Borodin's *Prince*

Igor. Gently, Daniel stayed her hand and selected 'Shangri-La' by the Kinks instead.

Daniel and Jack watched Mel carefully to see if she liked it. After a few bars, her face lit up. For Jack, the moment called to mind the first dinner he'd had at Juliet and Mel's house, as they watched nervously to see if he liked the food they lay before him.

It was more rewarding than he'd ever dared dream, this opportunity to share a life with another.

In the Cubby House, in the paddocks, by the creek, in the shed, Mel taught Jack about the classical composers and how to sing, and Jack taught Mel to draw.

Summer ended, and with it Miss Jackson's six weeks respite. She did not return, while Rush stayed on. Autumn passed by. Winter came next and with it – what could not be so relied upon – the rains. They flattened the grass, swelled the creeks, and greened the land.

Daniel seemed equally renewed, and politically engaged. To Jack and Mel, he outlined Whitlam's sweeping reforms. How the Prime Minister had abolished conscription. How he'd secured equal pay for women. Introduced no-fault divorce. Established a family court. Reduced the stigma around single mothers. Rolled out mothers' benefits and welfare for the homeless. Provided federal funding to state schools. Set up social planning and community development initiatives. And brought Australia's sewerage network into the 20th century!

He'd also inaugurated free tertiary education. This made Daniel especially glad for Jack; for Mel too, if she and her mother stayed in Australia to enjoy it. And for Simon, of course, if he ever wished to take advantage of such forward-thinking.

Whitlam had prohibited the reinstatement of the death penalty. Stamped out legislative forms of racial discrimination. Initiated land rights for the dispossessed original inhabitants, the Aborigines.

His achievements weren't solely national. He'd turned about Australia's xenophobic foreign policy, through recognising China, granting Papua New Guinea its independence, and renegotiating a less servile relationship with the US.

He was also unusual in being a Prime Minister not engaged exclusively with sport. He'd established a national gallery, a council for the arts, and radio stations for the young, which Daniel would play for Jack and Mel. Under Whitlam's stewardship, the Australian film industry was also thriving. Whitlam believed that in the arts, not sport, could be found the true soul of a nation.

But perhaps most transformative of all, he'd brought into existence a free universal healthcare system. It was a truly democratic initiative that would no doubt become the envy of other first world nations like the US.

'God save any future government that tries to repeal *that* initiative,' declared Daniel.

Jack and Mel did not understand it all, but they were infected with Daniel's enthusiasm.

'Of course, that's why the opposition mongrels are being so obstructive,' he concluded, his old dourness reinfecting his tone. 'But I don't see *that* man giving up.'

One time, at Mel and Juliet's house, the three of them sitting in the lounge, with daylight streaming through the transom windows of coloured glass, Jack and Mel played the Kinks to Juliet. It was a startling touch for Juliet, this getting to know Daniel's tastes in music, and him of hers, through the intermediary of their kids. For what had their actual meetings totalled in these past months – a scant half day at most? It wasn't their musical interests alone, the two had gleaned of each other. They also shared political sympathies – indeed, were aligned on numerous topics and issues. Married, almost, in thought …

It was the oddest, most enjoyable, but also excruciatingly sad pattern, this communication through the medium of youth neither any more possessed.

Yet all the while, Juliet's fate preyed on her. Her imminent, inescapable fate. Every little pain, the slightest headache, the smallest dizzy spell, she saw as a symptom. How soon till she would need Dash to move in? Had she asked too much of him?

Why wasn't she back in France with her friends? Mel, with hers? It would have been much simpler for Dash, too. He'd graciously complied with her last wish: to come home – *her* home, not his. But had Mel a friend in Paris to equal Jack? She looked at the large eyes of the two kids opposite her and realised she would need to speak before crying, before giving in.

Too soon. Too soon.

No, it wasn't over for her yet and she would still live while she might.

She leant forward on her mauve, tufted lounge, its threadbare state hidden under a slip cover, and addressed the two kids on the one opposite.

TOM CONYERS

'Jack, why don't you come to the opera tomorrow night with Mel, Dash and me? It's *Lakmé*, by Delibes.'

Mel pounced on the idea. 'Please, Jack. That's where I get my name.'

Jack's old hesitancy gone, but still some of his indecision remaining, he muttered, 'Yep. Okay.'

'And afterwards you can stay the night. Can't he, Mum? In the Cubby House?'

Jack's eyes lit up, but then a stricken look crossed his fair features. 'I'll ... I'll have to ask my mum.'

Dressed in a sheer black gown with her hair up, Juliet was glad no one had recognised her when they entered Don Dunstan's Festival Hall, and found their seats on one of the strange balconies, shaped like the rubber mouldings on sixties kitchenware. She'd never sung at the venue herself; Whitlam had only opened it two years earlier.

The orchestra finished warming up and the lights dimmed. The audience hushed as the royal red curtains parted.

A wonderful origami garden was revealed, resplendent with jade paper birds, the whole glade lit in dazzling colours. Mel watched with great interest as Lakmé, daughter of a Brahmin priest, sang with her servant – and Mel's namesake – Mallika, in an exquisite pairing.

'The famous 'Flower Duet',' her mother whispered beside her.

So the garden was known of before, Mel thought. And it would be known of again, no doubt, glimpsed through the door in the wall.

Alas, silly people in their English foppery invaded its sanctity, and Lakmé and Mallika fled. Lakmé re-emerged from a temple half-hidden among the foliage in an apricot dress, trimmed with cherry-red, to intercept the least absurd of the English gentry, Gerald.

Juliet had played the part of Lakmé five years earlier, in Vienna. Like the soprano before her, she too had been described as possessing a peerless legato, divinely controlled. But now she wondered if she should have sacrificed her mastery, teetered closer to the edge, and even gone over it. Considered a formidable talent, what heights might she have reached then, having now been acquainted with her imminent extinction, and the insights that brings?

The burgeoning love duet between Lakmé and Gerald touched her more acutely now than when she had sung it herself. The colour, the exoticism of this underrated opera! Each male part with its mellifluous arias, each female role with its ardent, sophisticated yearning.

Exuding confidence and strutting forth, Gerald began his persuasive seduction, with ascending and descending intervals, the inhalations and exhalations of an unquenched passion. Lakmé joined in and the irresistible seesawing in emotion was repeated, as their voices intertwined in long and longing flights, two souls briefly dovetailed. An aching, if imperfect, conjoining of souls.

Juliet gripped the arms of her seat, bumping Dash beside her. He, meanwhile, was embroiled in his own thoughts and emotions, equally inspired by the spectacle before him. Memories of past loves, both requited and spurned, wearily sought anchorage in his mind. It finally occurred to him how to explain to Mel why he and Juliet had not ended up together. As always with him, it would take the form of a story.

Juliet stopped herself gasping at the aria's termination, and looked down to see that tears also gemmed her daughter's eyes. They were each beset by a parallel grief. For Mel was gazing at the empty seat beside them. Jack's.

Chapter 12

Jack gazed down from his post on the Cunningham Casuarina outside his house to see Daniel pulling up in the station wagon. Jack had been humming the 'Flower Duet' in his head. Mel and Juliet had lent him the record, and he'd played it all afternoon in the shed.

The night was clear, with every visible star visible.

'Jack,' said Daniel, unpacking his station wagon, somehow sensing his son was perched above. 'Thought you'd be at Mel's?'

Jack said nothing as Daniel made his way to the front door where Jean had appeared, arms folded.

'Mrs Jeffries wanted to take Jack to the opera,' she explained tersely.

Daniel cocked his head.

'With her *lover*!'

A small flame of jealousy shot up in Daniel but he suffocated it almost instantly. If nothing else, he would not give in to this systemic pettiness. 'Oh well, bit of sing-song,' he shrugged, kicking off his boots.

'I'm not having them turn him into a ... well ...'

Daniel looked at her sharply. 'Oh, Jean.'

Jean was silenced by the staggering disappointment on his face. A disappointment, a weariness, so profound, it almost made her question her words. This stolid patience of Daniel's! She quickly stalked inside. Daniel stepped off the paving in his socks, and padded up to the trunk's base.

'You'd better start your homework, son. School tomorrow.'

Reluctantly, Jack swung down, and the two walked companionably towards the house. Suddenly Daniel stopped, having remembered something. He pulled a letter from his overall's pocket.

'Oh, I forgot. Your mother wanted me to give you this letter this morning. It's for Mr Higgins. We're having a barbecue at the weekend.'

Jack looked at the sealed letter.

Daniel smiled. 'Don't tell your mum I forgot now, will you, son?'

Jack took the letter, his mind focused on that word his mum had been about to use. He knew what it was because she'd finished other sentences with it in, and Simon made frequent use of it too.

Sissy.

Did a love of stories, music and the arts make him a candidate for that name?

'Jack,' said his father gently, and Jack stepped inside.

The next morning, Higgins, seated at his desk in his office, took the sealed envelope from Jack. He opened it with a silver letter opener and glanced at its contents.

'Oh, lovely. Tell your mother I'd be delighted to attend.' Jack turned to leave.

Higgins looked down at his hands thoughtfully then at Jack with a serious expression on his face. 'Oh, Jack, can I see your exercise book?'

Jack stopped in his tracks. Although he didn't understand all that fuss with his drawing, he had hoped it was at least forgotten. He hated that he now nursed an odd feeling about something he'd previously only felt pride in. And that feeling about his gift was … shame. Irritably, he slowly trudged back to Higgins' desk, opened his bag, and handed over his exercise book. He watched, fidgeting, as Higgins licked and thumbed each page till he got to *the* page, the one with the revised charioteer.

'Hmm, this is actually quite good.' Higgins scrutinised Jack suspiciously. 'You drew this?'

Jack sighed with exasperation. It was such a silly question; it was *his* exercise book, wasn't it?

'Of course.'

Higgins pursed his lips, got up from behind his desk, walked to the front of it and put a hand on Jack's shoulder.

'Don't lie, Jack.'

Something snapped in Jack.

'I *did* draw it!'

'Jack!' yelled Higgins, offended to the core by the boy's impudence. 'Sit down!'

Jack obeyed, reluctantly. Higgins walked to the sash window to calm himself, and peered through the glass.

The kids were rolling in outside, generation after generation. How many would he, Higgins, see through the revolving door, before the wheel of life completed its revolution for him?

Still gazing outside, he said more softly, 'Jack, I know your father used to paint pictures before he painted houses.'

Jack glanced up from his exercise book, which he was scribbling in with a pen he'd taken from Higgins' desk. What a stupid thing to say. While Daniel played with him in most games, he refused to engage in drawing or painting himself.

'Dad can't draw.'

Higgins tapped on the glass; no doubt a student outside was running or some other such misdemeanour, Jack thought wryly.

Higgins cleared his throat. 'When he met your mum, he was a doodler just like you. But doodling doesn't support a wife and kids.'

Jack digested this information. Daniel had never said he *couldn't* draw … just that it *hurt* somehow. Jack resumed his drawing.

Higgins still had his back to him.

'Don't dream your life away like your father. You could be one of our best students, Jack. Others might come and go. These city girls – *kids*, I mean – with all their airs. Miller's Creek Comprehensive might only be small, but I have always prided myself on giving every child who comes to this school a solid grounding.'

Higgins turned, his eyes adjusting to the dimmer interior light and stepped towards Jack.

'Therefore I expect the truth from each and every ...'

Higgins made a 'tsk' sound, disappointed to see Jack doodling again, when he had sermonised on just that topic.

'So you mustn't lie to me, Jack. You mustn't – ' He stopped, peering over the boy's bent head.

The *bastard!* Higgins pushed Jack back, ripping the offending page from the exercise book.

Surprised and afraid, Jack got up and retreated to the entrance door.

'Out,' was all Higgins could utter.

When left alone, Higgins dared un-scrunch the paper. Yes, it was unmistakably a caricature of him … in a nappy … sucking his thumb. The worst of it was, he knew it would not sting so acutely were there not a kernel of truth in it. The kid had seen unsympathetically into his soul.

Jack was in a dark mood, singing in his head the Kinks' 'I'm Not Like Everybody Else'. He was at a desk in the school library, which was hemmed between rows of metal bookshelves, all plated khaki green.

He was defacing his revised drawing of the charioteer, putting blood splotches here, blood splotches there, arms being lopped off. First one, then another, of his classmates, attracted no doubt by the sight and sound of him scribbling so furiously, had gathered to peer over his shoulder, till there was quite the crowd. Miss Ashton, the librarian with a bob cut, dark glasses, and precise small movements from always putting away books, glanced through the gap in the shelves between F and G at the strange throng.

Naturally timid, she hoped the kids would either disperse of their own accord or that the teacher meant to be supervising them would appear and put them in order.

Jack finished his revision by drawing an enormous penis on the charioteer. This elicited a raucous laugh from the other children, including Mel.

Their mouths shut as one.

His stomach dropping, Jack followed their gaze. Rush, a discoloured linen-bound book of Greek myths in his hand, was standing in front of them.

He surveyed the children before removing his reading glasses and theatrically craning his entire body from the waist down till his head was hovering over Jack's exercise book, his eyes a mere ruler's length from its open pages.

Rush recoiled slightly in surprise before removing his glasses and taking one last squiz of Jack's picture to make sure he'd seen correctly. He put his book under his left armpit the better to fog up then clean his glasses with a purple silk handkerchief.

Jack, by this stage, would have all but slipped under the table if it hadn't been jammed up against his chest from the other kids pressing behind him.

Many worries and thoughts crowded in on his mind, but the worst was whether this might be communicated to Juliet, and Jack's friendship with Mel threatened as a result.

Rush put his glasses back in his pocket.

'My, Jack, that's an unfortunate-looking penis,' he quipped before walking off, head back in book once more.

Miss Ashton, who was still spying between the gap in F and G, hit her head on the above shelf, dislodging several books, all of which she somehow managed to catch in a juggling motion without making the slightest sound.

'You've had it now,' Glen gloated over Jack's shoulder.

Jack looked up at the sea of faces. 'What's he gonna do?'

Emma chimed in. 'Tell Mr Higgins, I bet!'

Mel, who until then had thought the whole matter rather harmless, noted the worry on Jack's face. It was slick with perspiration.

'No, he won't,' she rejoined hastily.

Jack's eyes locked hers. 'Mel, do you think he'll tell my mum?'

Mel was already reassessing the adequacy of her concern, judging from not only the consternation on Jack's face but her classmates around her. She felt fairly sure what Dash would do (they'd agreed not to call him Dash at school to avoid 'rocking the boat') but she wasn't so sure of Higgins' response should he find out.

Mel looked worriedly at Rush, who was now sitting in the beanbag in the corner by the window, reading the book of Greek myths. She turned back to Jack. Was it something Dash would tell Higgins?

With library over, the kids piled back into their homeroom class. Mel sat at her and Jack's new spot up front, before discovering that Jack was hesitating to join her. Hearing Rush whistling as he brought up the stragglers, Jack pulled his head into his shoulders and made straight for the back.

'Jack!'

'I don't want him to see me, Mel. Maybe if I sit at the back, he'll forget.'

Mel got up promptly. 'I'll sit with you.'

'No,' said Jack, rather more loudly than he intended, but Rush's dark mop of wavy hair was looming into view at the door, and he had no time to be polite.

'No?' questioned Mel.

Jack leant in and hurriedly whispered. 'No, Mel. Maybe I should sit with Michael. I don't want to be called a … a sissy.'

When Jack stumbled into his old seat, Michael looked up and smiled, happy to have company again.

Mel sat down, hurt. Kate entered class, the last of the female stragglers, and eyeballed Mel contemptuously when she saw there was nowhere else to sit but next to her.

Rush was about to enter class when a large bear-like hand stopped him.

'Frank?' said Rush, surprised.

Higgins shot a glance at a few boys still entering class.

Rush corrected himself, amused. Placing the appellation of Mr or Mrs before a surname, or even a Sir or Miss, did not necessarily bring with it a student's respect. Personally, he wished everyone called him Dash, no matter their age.

Nonetheless, taking his own advice that he'd dished out to Jack and Mel before the holidays were over – not to 'rock the boat' – he smartly corrected himself.

'*Mr* Higgins.'

Higgins reached for the collection of Greek myths in Rush's hands, which Rush reluctantly relinquished. Higgins made a show of reading the cover before flipping through the pages without reading them.

'Mr Rush, don't you think some of the stories you tell in class are inappropriate for primary school children?'

Rush felt a tightening of his mouth. 'Inappropriate?'

'Yes,' said Higgins. 'Now, why not tell something from the good book?'

Higgins pulled a large, leather-bound tome from his voluminous coat pocket.

Rush stared at it a moment, reading the title. Reluctantly, he took the bible. He then held out his other hand for the book of Greek myths.

Higgins concealed it behind his back.

Rush flushed with anger.

Higgins smiled.

'I'll return it to the library for you.'

Higgins about-turned and loped back down the corridor and towards his office.

The anger had subsided in Rush, but he couldn't help feeling perturbed by the incident.

He entered class and noted that Jack and Mel were not sitting together. His unease at Higgins' behaviour swelled slightly at this further oddity, till he decided the two incidences could in no way be connected. His eyes travelled from Jack, who seemed weirdly like a tortoise trying to hide in its shell, and settled on Mel, straight and erect of carriage as always. She shrugged.

The lightness of that very gesture, the warmth and humour of it, buoyed him in a second. He would not be bested. He never had been.

Slowly, he leafed through the bible as the kids wondered at his uncharacteristic taciturnity. He stopped flipping suddenly, at Matthew 19:20, which he then proceeded to paraphrase in a tone more solemn, more serious, than the kids were used to from him. His characteristic pacing, however, was still very much in exhibition.

'There was once a rich man who owned a vineyard. One morning, he hired several labourers to pick grapes. At midday, he went out and hired several more. Then, late in the day, he hired a final group of workers. When it came time to pay the labourers their wages, those who started early in the day expected more pay than those who started later, and yet the man gave equal, generous pay to all. "Why?" they asked. "It is not fair that they that worked less should be paid as much as those who worked longer." "Can I not do as I like with my own money?" replied the rich landowner. "Why be jealous of my kindness?" Thus will the last be first, and the first last.'

Rush finally stopped pacing and gazed at the class. 'What might that be about, do you think?'

Glen, who was leaning back in his chair, and who had been influenced by his father talking about the oddity of the new teacher, said to elicit a response from his classmates, 'Getting ripped off!'

There was a dull laugh, which did not seem to disturb Rush. Mel noted he had that sparkle back in his eye.

'Ah,' he said, his voice alive and animated once more; finger raised. 'But they all got paid well in the end. Some worked longer for their money, though. What might you substitute the money for? Could this story really be about something else?'

Jack looked up from his desk, the parable having drawn him in. He'd listened to it avidly but he had also been thinking about what Mel had done earlier. She'd offered to sit at the back of class with him. He'd been wrong to rebuff her because he now saw it was her return gesture for him accompanying her to detention. And the fact she'd unhesitatingly reciprocated had flooded his heart with a joy not even his worry could extinguish.

Mel raised her hand.

'Yes, Mel?'

'Satisfaction?'

Rush smiled encouragingly. 'Perhaps, but what about ...'

'Love.'

Rush shot him a look. 'Yes, Jack, love. Some find it early in life, some later, but the reward is always the same.'

Jack blushed; he had not meant to say that out loud.

Mel raised her hand. Jack laughed inwardly – she might as well keep her hand up, she knew all the answers!

Rush gestured for her to speak.

Glancing over her shoulder at Jack, she answered in a chastising tone, 'Some people never find it at all.'

A sadness flashed over Rush's face. 'Ah alas, Mel, I think that's true.'

Jack felt even more ashamed for rejecting something as magical as a person wanting to stand alongside him, to form a windbreak against the travails of life.

Chapter 13

They rode home, Mel still not talking to him. Jack decided to hang back a good ten paces. Mel had already been upset with him for not coming to the opera. The ticket cost a whopping seventy dollars, she'd told him, which he'd squandered. But what could he have done when his mother wouldn't let him go? Eleven-year-old boys going to the opera – it would turn him into a … and there, again, was that word of which she was so fond.

If Daniel hadn't been out late with work, he would have argued the case. Jack had heard the two shouting late into the night, which was a welcome relief only in that it was a contrast from the tepid exchanges or mute passages. Jean often goaded Daniel to fight with her, but he almost never did. Last night had been a troublesome exception in that *he'd* started the shouting. 'How could you deny Jack the glimpse of a larger world?' Daniel railed.

Jack, hidden under his blankets, had felt nauseous to think such anger resulted from him.

They who worked longer in the vineyard were paid as much as those who only worked a short time.

Observing his own parents, and the strange, strained connection between Juliet and Dash, it occurred to Jack just how incredibly lucky he and Mel were to have found work in the vineyard so young.

Jack was brought back to the present when Mel sped through her open gate just as he stopped to unlock his.

When he got home, no one was there. He checked for a note on the fridge.

Jack, your mother and I have gone to watch Simon at footy training. Dinner's in the fridge.
Dad

Jack stared at it.
What else might the story be about?
Love, he'd whispered.
So what if Daniel and Jean fought about him?
Some people never find it at all.
Hadn't he a right to a friend?
Ah, alas, Mel, I think that's true.
He penned a note of his own, tacked it to the fridge with a ladybug magnet, and darted into his room.

He grabbed a knapsack, filling it with pyjamas and a sleeping bag. He then took the record he'd bought from behind his chest of drawers, where it had been hidden. Stuffing it into his knapsack, he hastily exited, going via the bathroom for his toothbrush.

Juliet was sitting under the back pergola, which was covered in vines and the odd spider web that must have been too high, even with a broom, to reach and brush away.

She was in her dressing gown, although a more elegant example than Jack had seen before, and her hair hung lank from a recent shower. She was still beautiful, but haunted somehow. Her eyes opened.

'I thought I heard Puck in my garden.'

Jack apologised for the previous night. She refused his offer to reimburse her for the ticket. (Not that he knew how – he would have to ask Daniel.)

'Keep the record,' she said before pointing in the direction Mel had wandered.

He at last found Mel in a spot the two rarely frequented; the opposite fence-line to the one they shared. There was a slight depression with a copse of trees, and remnants of an earlier boundary, a crumbling fence-line made of hand-sawn wood.

Mel was tipping an imaginary hat at the fence posts.

'Evening, Mozart … Howdy, Tchaikovsky ...'

At the third post, she paused solemnly, and nodded a greeting. 'Chopin.'

She resumed her step, expecting another post, but Jack had emerged from the shadow of the trees and was standing there instead.

'Well, hi ...?'

'Borodin.'

Mel smiled her pixie smile, forgiving Jack in an instant.

Jack titled his own imaginary hat and executed a magnificent bow. 'And hi ...?'

After a thoughtful pause, Mel said, 'Beethoven.' She had recently become obsessed with his *Moonlight Sonata*.

'Well, come hither, Beethoven, let us chargeth to the Cubby House.'

Mel cocked her head. 'The Cubby House?'

Jack held up his knapsack and sleeping bag. 'I'm staying over.'

Jack bounded off in the direction of the Cubby House. Mel stood dazed. What about always having to ask his mum's permission, which was so rarely granted? Jack paused and called to her.

'Beethoven? Beethoven! Are you deaf?'

Despite herself, Mel laughed at his joke. She ran after him to beat him on the head.

Daniel, Jean and Simon weren't surprised this time to return from Simon's footy practice and find no lights on in the house.

Jean beat Daniel and Simon inside and pranced straight to the fridge. Her fingers traced over the words of the note. With a start, she pulled it off the fridge, sending the ladybug magnet flying, and read it out to Daniel.

Mum and Dad, gone to Mel's. Be back tomorrow.
Jack.

With a small cry, Jean shredded the note in her hands. 'We can't let him, Dan!'

Daniel sighed. 'I guess. Not unless it's okay with Juliet.'

Jean threw up her hands. 'You know that's the least of my worries. But staying the night?'

'Jean! Really?'

Daniel wondered how they'd ever come to get married. He was sure Jean must have speculated on that matter herself, over the years. Neither had been paired off in their late teens. Heading into their twenties, they were the only guy and girl in town still left unmatched. Although striking, Jean had been too intimidating for the men; Daniel, considered a dish, had perplexed the numerous girls who asked him out on dates with his painful taciturnity.

His and Jean's pairing had been a match made by elimination.

Daniel regarded Jean tiredly.

'They're eleven, Jean.'

Jean was not satisfied. Daniel offered to ring Juliet.

'Since you're obviously still on such good terms, perhaps you can tell her to send Jack back. At once!'

'Oh, no trouble at all,' said Juliet over the phone.

Daniel rang off and turned to Jean, shrugging. He was expecting to be harangued for capitulating so easily, but Jean stopped pacing and shrugged in turn.

'Well, what's to worry about? He's only eleven.'

Daniel felt he could give her a smile.

'If Mel was with my Simon now ... well!'

His smile vanished.

She put her hand on Simon's shoulder, and shook it roughly.

'Aw, Mum!' said Simon, not liking the pressure she was putting him under.

She headed off briskly, as if that were that.

Daniel walked to the window, looking at the light in Mel's house. Simon's voice rang out behind him, the tone unmistakably sarcastic.

'So, Dad, who'd have thought? Little Jacko's got a girrrl-friend.'

Daniel remained staring at that hamlet of light under a vast, starry and mostly, he felt, loveless sky.

'So it seems,' he whispered.

In the same house, a quarter of a century earlier, he had sketched, painted, while she had danced, sung.

He headed for bed, pausing in front of Simon with a sudden, brilliant smile on his face. 'Lucky kid, eh?'

With his father gone, Simon shot a glance at Mel's house. He found himself chewing the side of his mouth. What did Jack have that was absent in him? Or … different? Simon feared that he was in his own way as unusual as his brother. This perception led to another: 'weakling' Jack actually harboured a quiet inner strength. Did he, Simon, share that courage or was it in him mere bravado?

He shuddered, admitting to himself he was afraid.

Night had bathed the world in a rich, dark blue. There was the faintest sound of wind gently caressing the trees, petting the grass.

Jack and Mel were sitting in their pyjamas in the Cubby House, facing each other. Jack was holding his temples, concentrating. Mel was staring at a handmade card with a cross drawn on it, which she was keeping hidden from Jack's view, like a fabulous poker hand.

'What are you getting?' she asked impatiently.

Jack rubbed his temples with his forefingers like she'd instructed him to do, scrunched his eyes closed all the tighter and tried – tried with all his significant powers of imagination – to mentally receive the image on the card Mel was transmitting with her thoughts. At least, that's how he thought the game went.

'Nothing,' he said at last.

Mel threw down the card, which landed face up.

'Damn.'

Jack noted the cross. He hadn't 'received' the faintest tinge of that.

'Mel, this is stupid.'

'No it's not. The Russians did it. They sent thoughts across Siberia.'

So *that's* what she'd been reading about. She was always coming up with some new exotic activity, which mostly Jack enjoyed. But this time …

'Well, *we're* right next to each other,' he pointed out.

Mel closed her eyes patiently before reopening them and cupping his with her gaze.

'Only some people can do it. Only those who really know each other. And only with one person. Once in a lifetime or never at all. Now, how about *you* send the pictures? You're better at that than I am.'

Mel shuffled through the pack the way she'd seen Juliet's European circle do at Bridge club. She closed her eyes while Jack pulled out a card. He put it down flat on the blanket, as instructed, and started concentrating. He imagined the circle forming as a spinning hoop in his head, gaining in size and increasing in revolutions, till it popped from his brain like a smoke ring he'd seen some of the men outside the pub blow. Only, this was a fiery ring, which he imagined burning through Mel's forehead and into her brain.

'A circle?' Mel offered tentatively.

Jacks eyes flicked open. 'Yes!'

'Balls.'

'No, really.'

Mel cocked her head. 'Really?'

Jack nodded solemnly. 'I promise.'

Mel smiled. 'Cross your heart?

Jack thumped his thigh. 'Cross my heart, hope to die, stick ten thousand needles in my eye.'

'Never promise to die, Jack!' she scolded him. Her face relaxing, she beamed herself. 'That's fantastic. We're telepathic.'

'What's that mean?'

Mel got all serious once more. 'Well, tele – like TV. And pathic ... um ... Quick, do another one. Write it down this time, and don't cheat!'

The accusation of cheating stung Jack. It reminded him too painfully of the incident with Higgins. Well, he had shown Higgins and now he would show her. Petulantly, Jack shuffled the cards and picked another. He then placed it face down on the doona. Unlike before, he had the new shape created in his head and popped into hers in seconds.

'A square?' Mel ventured uncertainly.

Jack affected nonchalance. Leaning back on his hands, he watched Mel flip the card over.

'Blinkety Bill!'

Excited at this strange, strange world unfolding before them, the two continued, their pace not slacking. Symbol after symbol Jack successfully sent and Mel just as successfully picked up on.

'Nine in a row!' shouted Mel. 'That's amazing!'

Jack was not so enthused now; he was rubbing his head.

'Can we stop now, Mel? My head's aching.'

'All right, but let's – '

Mel was interrupted by Juliet calling from below.

'Mel, Jack? Hadn't you best go to sleep now?'

'All right, Mum!' yelled Mel.

Jack covered his ears. She certainly had a powerful set of lungs. Would she end up a singer like Juliet?

Mel got up and went into the antechamber, thrusting her head down the manhole. 'Is Dash here yet?'

Jack became slightly uneasy. Rush – how would he face him after the episode in the library?

'I thought he was coming tonight,' said Juliet. 'Perhaps he got caught up.'

The friends lay quietly, each knowing the other had not yet drifted off. Jack was thinking about the telepathy cards. He knew who must have introduced Mel to them: Rush. He'd already taught them so many things in a way that was so subtle it didn't seem like teaching at all. The imagination ... the imagination as a way to see the world better.

'You're lucky to see so much of Mr Rush outside of school,' said Jack.

Mel immediately sat up, as if she'd been waiting for just that cue.

'There's something I must tell you.'

Jack knew. After all, they could read each other's minds.

'He's your dad.'

Mel nodded.

Yet something remained unclear to Jack, something Mel kept hidden. 'Then why aren't they together?'

'He isn't ... it isn't my place to tell, but ...'

Jack smiled encouragement in the semi-darkness. Mel continued.

'He and mum weren't meant to be but ...'

'... *you* were,' Jack finished for her.

Mel blushed but then got serious again. 'Well, if *you* don't mind about him, Jack, *I* don't mind. I won't ever mind about anything so long as you're at my side.'

Jack had no intention of ever being elsewhere. How few found each other, how lucky were he and Mel! In such a wide world, with so many millions, that he should meet her, and she, him ... the luck of it! He intuited Mel had thought the same but perhaps neither dared articulate this amazing fact of their finding each other for superstitious fear it could be undone. Yet how can magic be uncast, a spell dispelled?

But then I knew that very soon you'd leave me

That damned melancholy of the Kinks! No, he knew the melancholy was not of the Kinks' making but already present in the world. The Kinks were only exceptionally skilled at bringing it out. He wouldn't let their cynicism get the better of him all the same, and pushed it down.

Mel was gently laughing at the contortions his thoughts were no doubt rendering to his face.

'We're very wide awake, the moon and I,' she sang.

And Jack knew her greatest gift.

She would show everyone:

The world could be so good.

Sometime in the night, Jack woke with the possums scurrying across the corrugated iron roof, no doubt using it as a bridge between the branches of the trees enclosing it. They were pretty things, with their small twitching noses and glittering eyes, but there was nothing pretty about the screeching noises they could make.

He rolled on his side to see Mel's unmoving back in the dark. How could she sleep through such a racket? Then he remembered her telling him how their previous home, a flat in Austria, fronted a main street with trolleys rattling past, cars, trucks, noisy revellers. Those man-made sounds would wake her, but nothing in the country had, except the almost personally welcoming call of the birds in the morning, sheep bleating and cows lowing, and Jack's rooster from down the hill.

Something caught his eye through the window. There was a shape on the branch outside, the inverted teardrop of an owl. It moved its head silently to regard him, its shoulders and head outlined in white from the blue moon.

He stood slowly so as not to startle it and pressed himself against the cold glass, his breath fogging it up. Wiping it with his pyjama sleeve, he spied through a gap in the trees a sparser-leaved tree down a ways on the hill, its trunk a lonely, pasty white against a deep blue-black sky.

Jack recalled Mel's words from their first sojourn between each other's properties.

'Well, it's lonely. Even the trees are lonely. If I … *died* here, though, the trees would have me for company.'

The owl took to the air in a noiseless flap. Shuddering, Jack got back in his sleeping bag and inched closer to Mel.

He woke again, just before dawn. He got up with an energy he'd never before mustered so early, and peeped through the window. There was the very faintest tinge of light purpling the sky beyond the hill as the heavens paled with dawn.

Making sure not to wake Mel, he grabbed the Grieg record from his backpack, slipped the disk from its plastic sleeve and placed it on the record player. Conveniently, the track he was after was first. Pressing the button, the needle arm jarringly swung into position before dropping and finding the groove.

Grieg's *Morning Mood* trilled to life.

Mel woke with the first sunbeams shooting over the lip of the hills and refracting through their window, illuminating like sparks the motes and dust in the Cubby House.

She rose in one unstretching, fluid movement, joining Jack at the window.

The sun now fully breached the horizon, its beams like the spokes of a half-shattered wheel of a wagon, fanning across the land, the paddocks, catching the edge of the trees, separating each one with its moulding light. The mist burnt away with the warming of the land, revealing sheep rising from their huddles, lambs playing in the dewy grass, bulls unlocking their joints and sending them bellowing, while cows licked their calves, and calves suckled their mothers, and all made their way to the creek and dams for their morning drink.

Jack and Mel slipped on their sneakers, climbed down the rope ladder and wandered out to the frosted grass, the side of the Cubby House now bathed in a glorious golden light. All the while, the alternating flute and oboe of Grieg's piece played in their ears and then, once they were too far from the Cubby House to still hear it, in their heads and finally on their lips. Oboe, flute, bassoon, violin and cello merged together as in a pebbly stream, combining to a barely tamed ferocity of feeling, a veritable flood.

As Jack and Mel ran, danced and rolled in the dewy grass, not caring how wet they got, *Morning Mood* faded with the mist.

They made their way down to the creek, fringed with willows, choked in places with weeds and smelling of wild fennel.

Mel hit Jack lightly on the shoulder. 'You're it!'

'No, Mel,' protested Jack. 'Not *now*.'

But Mel had already disappeared among the trees. He searched for her, but in vain.

'Don't give up, Jack,' reverberated across the valley.

'Don't ever give up,' echoed, fainter and fainter.

Once more, Mel had simply vanished. Feeling sad and irritable, Jack turned for home, nursing the disturbing suspicion that perhaps these disappearances of hers were preparing him … but for what?

Chapter 14

The following morning, Jack was in his old seat at the back of class. He'd waited to ride with Mel but when she failed to show at the gate, he eventually got going so he wouldn't be late himself. It seemed she wasn't alone in her tardiness: the bell had rung a quarter of an hour ago and there was still no sign of Rush.

Mel entered finally and sat at their new spot at the front of class. She gave him a subdued smile over her shoulder. Jack was still annoyed with her vanishing act, but got up and joined her.

'Do you think Mr Rush has forgotten about my drawing?' he asked.

'Yes, silly.'

Jack sat down, breathing out slowly. He noticed Mel looked worried. He felt a sudden pang of concern.

'Why were you late?'

'Dash. Mum and I went round this morning, but he – '

The door opened. Instead of Rush, Higgins walked in, scowling. The class hushed immediately, and those still milling found their seats. Higgins said nothing; he merely put his briefcase on the desk. Mel and Jack exchanged glances. To Jack's instant panic, Higgins' eyes seemed to search out his.

Higgins broke the stare. 'Okay, class, I'm taking over today. Get out your books.'

Mel and Jack turned to each other again, worrying thoughts ricocheting between them. Higgins began writing on the blackboard. Jack noted sourly that he was copying from Miss Jackson's red notebook.

Before long, the clean blackboard became filled with Higgins' barely legible scrawl. At last, the recess bell rang and class was dismissed. As Jack tried to leave with Mel, Higgins grabbed his shoulder.

'Wait, Jack.'

Mel stopped, too.

'It's all right, Mel,' said Higgins. 'Off you go.'

Mel's eyes darted to her friend's, and she saw the fear in them.

'No,' she declared.

'Mel! I said leave!'

'Nothing will make me.'

Higgins' mouth opened and closed without sound. Just then, Jack spied through the classroom window his parents being ushered into Higgins' office by the secretary, Pauline. The fear liquefied in his stomach, swirling upwards towards his throat.

He stepped up to Mel. 'What about me, Mel? Can *I* make you go?'

Mel looked at him obstinately.

'Please?'

'Only you,' she said, at last. As Jack turned to accompany Higgins, he swallowed drily. Just what was all this about?

Jack was sitting one side of Higgins' large oak desk, between Daniel and Jean; Higgins had taken the head; and two adults Jack had never seen before were seated opposite him.

Pauline left and shut the door, having finished bringing in extra chairs.

Jack scrutinised the two strangers. Prue was mid-thirties, very thin, with tied-back strawberry hair and a pinched expression; Guy had a curly blonde beard and fair hair. He wore a khaki turtleneck.

'It's all right, Jack,' said Daniel, reading his son's anxious thoughts. 'These people just want to ask you some questions, that's all.'

Higgins nodded solemnly to Jean. To Jack's consternation, she reached into his knapsack and pulled out his exercise book, which she handed to Higgins.

'Mum?'

Higgins solemnly passed the exercise book to the social workers. The two briefly leafed through it, nodding and sighing in starts. The noises stopped when they came to the redrawn picture of the charioteer, complete with Jack's additional graffiti. Letting go of the half of the book she was holding, Prue leant forward, addressing Jack.

'What did Mr Rush talk about with you, dear?'

Jack's eyes darted round the table. What could Dash have to do with this? Daniel nodded that he should speak.

'Well ... we talked about dinosaurs and Mozart and about working different hours in the vineyard and getting the same pay. And about love – '

'Love?' Prue interjected.

'Um, yes,' continued Jack, hoping to get this out of the way. 'And about the Greeks, and the Olympics, and how they were in the ... nude ...'

Jack finished the sentence before he realised. His stomach roiled up: this was about *that* picture again!

Jean, Daniel and Higgins shared a worried look, Prue and Guy a triumphant one, as if they were finally getting somewhere. Prue leant forward.

'Did Mr Rush ever touch you?'

Jack watched Guy write something down. Why didn't that one talk?

Prue continued in her insistent murmur. 'Did he touch you, dear?'

Jack looked blank.

'Put his hands on you?'

Higgins drum-rolled his fingers. Jack scoped his parents. Jean was stern of feature, Daniel nodding kindly.

Jack recalled the time Rush put a hand on his shoulder when congratulating him on his drawing. Not the … *bad* drawing. The redrawn version, before Jack vandalised it, defaced his own work. Was that hand on his shoulder what they meant by touching?

Prue lowered her voice even further, yet there was now an insistent edge to it. 'Did Mr Rush touch you, Jack?'

Jack had looked up at Rush at the time.

He now looked up at Prue and Guy.

'Did he touch you?' repeated Prue, her voice rising.

Did they mean more by the term 'touch' than he understood in its meaning?

'I'm ... I'm not sure,' he said at last.

Prue leant back. She and Guy shared a jubilant grin, Daniel, Jean and Higgins a worried glance. Prue leant close to Guy's ear and whispered. He nodded and wrote something down on paper.

She leant towards Jack again, now somewhat embarrassed in her demeanour.

'Um, we believe Mr Rush asked you about your ... er ... willie?'

Jack stared at her blankly.

Prue cleared her throat.

'Um, your penis?'

Jack's face dropped. Why had he ever drawn that on his picture?

Mel had her head down, writing distractedly, in her seat at the front of the classroom. The door opened, and Jack entered with Higgins. Mel nodded urgently upfront. He followed her gaze to find that Miss Jackson was facing the blackboard, copying notes from her red book.

'Miss Jackson,' said Higgins, 'I'm sorry to have brought you back from your early retirement.'

Miss Jackson swivelled round, dusting the chalk off her hands. 'It was the least I could do, Mr Higgins. Under the circumstances.'

Higgins pushed Jack forward. 'I'll leave Jack with you.'

Jack walked in a daze towards Mel, barely noticing the door close behind Higgins. He was about to sit next to her when Miss Jackson barked in his ear, 'Jack!'

Jack jumped. Noticing for the first time that the class had once again been clearly divided into girls and boys, he turned from Mel and sleepwalked to the back to sit next to Michael. Satisfied, Miss Jackson endeavoured to continue writing notes but found herself fixated with something on the windowsill. She approached to examine her beloved plant, wilted from neglect, her lips compressing together. The class stole frightened glances at her as she watered it. Her eyes wandered down to the metal tray with the Jurassic sandpit. She picked up a paper palm that had fallen over, set it straight and then slowly counted the dinosaurs, aloud.

'One ... Two ... Three ... Four ... Four? Only four? There should be one more!'

Her beady eyes fell on the class. 'No one wants to own up?'

Not a single kid answered. For a rare moment, Miss Jackson wondered why she was scaring them, but then their obstinacy in not responding irked her afresh.

'Well, we're all staying here till someone does.'

Mel thrust up her hand. Miss Jackson regarded her, surprised.

'Can I look in the sand?' yawned Mel.

Miss Jackson's brow trampolined. Who was this daring young thing? '*Please*, Miss Jackson!'

Mel sighed. 'Ple-e-ase, Miss Jackson.'

Miss Jackson stared at the impudent girl with braids in her hair. Of all the kids before her, the new kid was the only one not trembling.

'All right,' Miss Jackson responded at last, oddly calm. 'Why not? You too,' she added, indicating Emma as well.

Emma looked at Mel as if to say, 'What have you gotten me into?'

The two got up and sifted through the sand in the diorama. Jack focused on their hands, like miniature bulldozer ploughs. His attention shifted to one particular palm tree, drawn there as if hypnotised. With a sudden turn of her head, Mel's eyes locked on his. Whilst still looking at him, she reached for the palm he was staring at, asking with a raise of her eyebrows if it were the right one. Jack nodded. Mel's fingers were about to close round it when Miss Jackson roared.

'Enough!' She leaned in to Mel, eyeballing her. 'No luck, eh?'

Angered, Mel again reached for the palm but Miss Jackson clapped her hands with such force that Mel retrieved her fingers as from a snakebite.

'Okay, enough you two.'

Again, Mel hesitated.

'*Sit*!'

Her ears ringing, Mel returned to her desk. Miss Jackson declared that since no one was going anywhere, they might as well all continue copying notes. The familiar scraping of chalk on blackboard resumed.

It became as insensate, as mindless, and as irritating to Jack as a branch tapping on a window, or an unlocked gate moaning in the wind.

He got up and made his way between the desks, focused solely on the palm. He brushed past Mel, who looked up in alarm, but he did not notice her. He reached for the sand tray.

The mad pecking of the chalk ceased.

'Jack, sit down! I didn't say you could get up. Sit down. Sit down at once!'

Jack turned his back on Miss Jackson and picked up the palm tree. Inside, as he somehow knew, was the missing dinosaur. He drew it out, turned round to Miss Jackson and held it up, triumphantly.

Miss Jackson groped for the metal ruler on the blackboard sill.

'I've found it!' declared Jack.

She whacked him across the ear, blood spurting across the front rows. The dinosaur dropped to the floor, rolling to her buckled shoes. She reached down and picked it up as Jack felt his piercingly hot, wet ear.

'*LIAR*!' screamed Miss Jackson. 'You had it in your pocket, didn't you, you naughty boy? You snuck it into the sand just then! I'm not stupid, you know, *you little shit*!'

Tears streamed down Jack's face. He tried to stop them with his sleeve, but they only flowed faster. Blood, snot and tears merged together, on his neck, on his clothes. As he reached up instinctively to his torn earlobe, the class gazed, astounded, as yet more blood welled between his fingers. Miss Jackson went to speak but restrained herself, realising for once she had gone too far. Noticing the blood now running down Jack's neck, she even felt fearful. What had she done? She stepped towards him in a consoling attitude, putting a hand on his shoulder.

Jack's tears ceased in a second. He beheld her hand a short moment before slapping it away with vehemence.

'*DON'T TOUCH ME*!' he yelled menacingly.

Miss Jackson stumbled backwards.

'Don't ever touch me again!'

She quickly sidestepped as Jack stormed out. Mel waited for a heartbeat, looked at Miss Jackson, then ran out after him. Miss Jackson turned to the class in a daze. Thirty faces stared back at her in fright and disgust. Michael hissed, his own treatment at her hands still fresh in his memory.

Chapter 15

Jack and Mel rode home without speaking, Mel this time the one to be hanging back. It was a quiet, contemplative ride, for they had left class a whole hour early, and there were no other kids to either pass or overtake them, either walking, on bikes, in cars, or on the school bus.

Arriving at their respective gates, Jack opened his and pushed his bike through as Mel offered to 'be a witness'. Jack merely brushed the flaky blood from his neck and pushed his hair over his ears. He saddled his bike and was already pedalling off when Mel called after him, 'She's lost, Jack!'

Jack braked and glanced over his shoulder. Why was Mel feeling sorry for *her*?

'But *we're* not, Jack. Don't you ever forget that.'

When he got home, everyone else was out. He cleaned up his ear then stepped outside to stare at that one island of joy and mystery in his life, the house enclosed in the wooded hamlet atop the hill.

He made his way through the ghost gums, avoided the gate to their garden, and slipped through the wires of the fence where it was closed in with trees. He gazed through the branches at the sagging veranda, remembering back to the first time he'd spied someone stepping out from under it: Juliet, when the Mitchell boys unloaded the last of her things.

Why was he spying now?

He could see Dash in his felt smoking jacket, Juliet in her long dress coat and Mel still in the clothes she'd worn to school. The three were standing talking on the chipped stone drive.

Jack gulped nervously before emerging from the wood to join them. Juliet stopped speaking, mid-sentence. Dash stepped back, palm raised.

'You shouldn't – you shouldn't come near me, Jack. Please get him away.'

Juliet stepped between them. 'Go away, Jack.' It was the first time she'd ever been short with him, and the pain of it cut deeply.

'But why? Why?' he asked.

'Please,' she insisted.

'But Mum!' cried Mel, grabbing Jack and holding him so he couldn't leave.

Dash looked like he might be about to cry, or had been crying. It troubled Jack deeply to see Dash so upset; because it occurred to him for the first time he had found something infinitely comforting in Dash's charismatic demeanour. Until then, he'd seemed immune from the world. But if this man, this cool, calm collected man, was in this state, what hope for him in life – a shy, timid boy?

Juliet pinned Jack with her eyes. 'Jack, why did you say that about Dash?'

Jack looked from one adult to the other.

'I didn't! I didn't say anything! They asked me questions. I didn't know what they were asking!'

Juliet's stiffness of manner somewhat thawed and she knelt down and took his shoulders. 'Jack, look at me. Only at me. Has Dash ever harmed you?'

Jack looked from Dash to Juliet. 'No. Never!'

Juliet and Dash shared a look.

'He seems just as surprised at the idea as I do,' said Dash, shaking.

Juliet stood and began pacing, slapping the side of her head in an uncharacteristically ugly gesture. 'This damned place! I should never have come back.'

Jack had never seen Juliet angry, either. He realised he was trembling himself, like Dash.

Abruptly, Juliet stopped pacing and took Mel's face in her hands. 'Darling, you know why Dash is here, don't you?'

Mel bit her lip. 'Because he's going to look after me for a while.'

Juliet swallowed. 'He's going to look after you *from now on*.'

'Mum?'

'I'm sorry, we'd hoped it might be here with you finding Jack. But you can see that's impossible now, can't you?'

Jack felt his heart fall out.

Juliet smoothed her hair. 'Come. Let's see Dash off to his cupboard.'

They stared at her. She waved her arms. 'Dash – to the cupboard! His cupboard!'

Juliet pointed at Dash's Valiant as if they were the ones who were confused.

'There! His cupboard!'

Mel trembled, her bottom lip wobbling. '*Car*, Mum. Dash's *car*.'

Juliet swung from them, gripping then smacking her head.

'Out, out! I want it out!'

Dash dissuaded Jack and Mel from following her, stumbling, into the house.

'This will all get sorted out … no need to worry,' he said, as he herded them to his purple Valiant.

Pausing at the door, he turned back, knelt, hugged then kissed Mel on both cheeks, and she, him, till they were giggling. When he stood, Jack stepped forward, arm raised for a handshake. Something in the way Rush stumbled back, made Jack stop short. The rebuff smarted keenly.

Appearing pained, Rush examined his hand then Jack's, still held, hopeful, in the air. Rush laughed and saluted instead.

'If I'm not able to see you again before I leave, Jack, you make sure you look us up on the continent, do you hear? I've a couple of contacts in the arts I'll put you onto. No giving up now.'

Dash sat in his car and tried to shut the door, but Jack had grabbed the handle.

'One more story. Please!'

Rush glanced between him and Mel. 'You can tell your own stories now. You two troopers always could.'

They watched the purple Valiant charger all the way down the long driveway, pass through the open gate, and turn left at the main road, disappearing among the broken hills.

'Goodbye, Doctor,' whispered Jack.

Dash was leaving, leaving on adventures far and wide, and would be taking Mel. While he, Jack …

The tears welled up and he ran. He ran all the way to the property on the other side of Juliet's, Mel chasing him.

She eventually caught him up and made him stop, the two panting together like spent foals in the grass tufts, so many blonde eyelashes.

Jack was mumbling to himself, 'Don't cry, Jack, don't cry.'

He tried to run again but Mel grabbed his shirt and wouldn't let go.

'Jack, wait. Jack, please wait.'

He wrested back his stretched shirt. 'I'll be stuck here, Mel,' he got out between violent sobs. 'Stuck without you. Dash lied. Nothing changes. We can't really travel in time.'

Mel regarded him seriously. 'Something *has* changed, Jack. We can read each other's minds.'

'Can we?' he threw off sceptically.

The tears flooded Mel's eyes too. 'That dinosaur – you told me where it was by nodding.'

Jack threw up his hands. 'Yes, by *nodding* to it!'

Mel was adamant. 'I *can* read your mind, Jack.'

Jack found his crying abating, anger replacing it. 'Don't lie to me.'

Mel was just as adamant. 'I would never lie to you, Jack. Never.'

'You *did* lie to me, Mel. You said your dad was a spy!'

Mel's mouth shut. After a long moment, she spoke. 'Mum told me why my dad and she couldn't be together. The reason … well, I thought that made him a bad person. That's why neither told me Dash was my father till I got to know him. I'm so ashamed I ever denied he was my father now. I couldn't have asked for a better dad.'

'If I had a dad like Dash, I would never be ashamed,' said Jack.

'Daniel's a great dad, too,' she said.

'But he's so shy, so … and I'm taking after him!'

'Mum says lots of guys came back from fighting in Vietnam like that.'

Daniel fought in Vietnam?

Jack reached down inside himself and realised he'd always known this too. He wondered if perhaps we all start off knowing everything, and then forget what's real, what matters, from the prison of maddening dreams: our waking lives.

But if Daniel had fought in Vietnam, what was Jack's excuse?

Mel reached out to touch him but he pulled away. Angry with himself, he wiped his eyes with his sleeve.

'Look at me, crying in front of a girl.'

Mel's face collapsed in great heaving sobs and Jack felt a searing shame come over him. What an idiot he was! Mel was soon to lose so much more than him. He reached out and, for the first time, took her hand.

The two walked along the undulating hills in silence, till they had gone beyond either's property, to the base of Mount Miller itself. This, they climbed, just as silently, helping each other up steep banks, over tumbled rocks, and finally to the very peak, where the world opened up in every direction.

Jack began humming the first few bars of *Polovtsian Dances* in his head. Mel then sang the next few out loud.

Jack spun round to her, in raptures, Mel nodding as if to say, 'See, we *can* read each other's minds.'

Jack felt a surge of inexpressible joy, and hugged her, pointing to a collection of boulders.

'Can you see it?'

The rocks reformed.

'Saint Basil's Cathedral,' she declared.

The two danced between the rocks, now walls; through trees, now pillars; past logs, now pews; and finally came to a halt in front of a great, upward jutting shaft of granite, now a magnificent organ in their re-imagined cathedral of nature.

'I've found you,' they both cried.

At the dinner table with his family, no one speaking, Jack played with his food. The phone rang. Daniel rarely got calls so he remained seated. When Jean likewise did not make a move to answer it, Daniel got up and took the call himself.

It was Juliet, sounding short and strained. She wanted Jack to come over. When Daniel questioned whether that was wise, she cut him off and explained tiredly that, no, Dash was not there; no, none of them would be there soon; and yes, the town had won and Daniel and Jean could have their lonely little hamlet back.

When Daniel rang off and relayed the situation, Jean said no.

Daniel resumed eating. The silence continued until he brought his hand down hard on the table, the cutlery and glasses jumping.

'Let him stay the night, damn you!'

Jean turned her stony face to him. Simon and Jack shrunk into their seats. Unable to bear another moment, Jack grabbed his knapsack and ran out the front door, not even closing it behind him.

The Cubby House window caught the last of the daylight before the sun crouched below the trench of night.

Inside, Jack and Mel were giggling, drawing, the shaded light flickering overhead. The moths fluttered like pleasant, insistent thoughts. Mel kept drawing over Jack's work till soon their lines were chasing each other. Normally, Jack liked his pictures executed with neatness and clarity. This time, he was happy for messiness.

'I still don't understand about Dash,' Jack said. 'If ever two people seem like they should be together ...'

Mel smiled warmly. 'He was right.'

Jack cocked his head.

'Dash! We *can* tell our own stories.'

She got up and put on Tchaikovsky's *Swan Lake*. Jack had heard Tchaikovsky's sonorous, swelling sounds before, with his *Piano Concerto No. 1*, but this was something else and beyond.

'Will this answer my question?' he asked, amused.

'Shoosh!' said Mel, and began to narrate her tale. 'In a dimly lit but stately room in Saint Petersburg, Russia, a secret "court of honour", presided over by none other than the Tsar himself, gathers to sentence a certain Pyotr Ilyich Tchaikovsky. The year is 1893.'

Jack felt himself enclosed in a brilliantly ornate room where serious, bearded gentlemen in fussy attire were gathered. The music, meanwhile, had quickly become a carousel of emotion, a swirling, building, collapsing epiphany of beauty and intense, passionate feeling.

'You see,' whispered Mel, shining a torch under her chin, 'Tchaikovsky had tried marriage, but had not been happy and made the woman he was with miserable too. But he had found love eventually, he had been rewarded for his work in the vineyard, when he fell into the arms of a nephew of a powerful duke.'

Mel conjured for Jack a dim cloistered room where the dapper Tchaikovsky and handsome duke held hands on a divan. But then the door burst open, and in ran armed police.

The notes seesawed with an almost sickening intensity of feeling, a feeling so bloated Jack wondered how it might spend itself.

Mel killed the electric light so now only the moon and the torch lit her face. 'Tchaikovsky was given an ultimatum: take arsenic or face public exposure and humiliation!'

She flicked off her torch as the music swung upwards, a first cantering, then galloping, hoof-fall of aching vitality.

Jack saw Tchaikovsky in a room with all the blinds drawn, a light from above falling on his head, while a faceless figure proffered him a goblet of plashing liquid as a ring of cloaked figures stepped from the darkness.

Mel flicked back on the torchlight, shining it under her chin. 'Tchaikovsky's lover sits in the audience at a performance of *Swan Lake*, surrounded by the shadowy figures and other members of the Tsar's court.'

Jack felt himself on the precipice of a theatre balcony, overlooking a stage of swirling, pirouetting dancers. Next to him, he espied the nephew of the duke, leaning forward, wringing gloved hands.

'As Tchaikovsky died painfully of what was passed off as cholera, the Tsar and his court listened to the music of not only Russia's greatest composer, but one of the greatest composers of all time!'

Jack watched in abundant horror and misery as the tears ran down the cheeks of Tchaikovsky's lover, the music soaring to its final expression of longing, before turning and endlessly retreating, like an unceasing tide.

Mel clicked her fingers. Jack stared at her. Her story had drawn him in so completely, and he fully understood its meaning. He speculated if perhaps in time he might illustrate her stories, that storytelling was the foremost talent she possessed, that united they could wow the world.

If Rush had boyfriends, that didn't seem so bad to Jack. He'd wanted a male friend himself till Mel came along and he found out girls could like science fiction, too.

For the first time he'd known her, Mel appeared shy, almost vulnerable.

'You'll still … me and Dash … I mean, will you …'

'Visit you two in Europe?' Jack threw a pillow at her. 'Try stopping me!'

It was nearly time for bed. Both luxuriated in their yawning. And yet they dallied in turning off the light altogether, for when might they experience this again, wrapped in blankets and open sleeping bags, the stars outside winking?

Jack found himself humming 'Days'.

Mel sat up. 'Not *that* song.'

'You don't like that song?'

'I *love* it. I love it! Only…' She looked around then whispered a line from it:

But then I knew that very soon you'd leave me

So she was troubled by it too? But they'd found each other. They'd found each other and Jack knew neither would ever willingly let go.

The image of the 'unhappiness brigade' from Mel's Tchaikovsky story flickered across Jack's mind. He knew it still existed. He knew it had never *not* existed. His father had hinted it would bring down Whitlam too.

Mel brought out the cards for their telepathic exercises and showed Jack. 'Shall we?'

Jack looked at them. The concentration needed ... he was tired.

'We can always ring each other, you know,' he joked.

Mel fixed her eyes on him forlornly. 'Perhaps not ... where *I'm* going.'

Jack did not wish to refuse her, so he sat up, massaging his temples 'to get the lobes working'. Something like that – he didn't know the technical language.

Mel shuffled the cards. 'I tried sending you one last night.'

'You!' he scoffed.

Mel tried to be offended. 'You're not the only one good with pictures.'

Indeed, her skills in that area had increased, just as his had in music and singing.

She picked a card, making sure not to let Jack see, then imitated his temple-rubbing routine while he dropped his hands and closed his eyes, with her concentrating on sending, him on receiving.

After a long moment, he unscrewed one eye. 'A square?'

Mel showed him the card. 'Yep. Like you.'

She picked another card and tried sending it as well.

'Circle.'

'Yep.'

'What goes round, comes around,' said Jack. 'Nothing changes.'

Mel drew another card, the cross, but hesitated. Something about picturing that cross burning through the front of her head and into Jack's caused her to shiver. Seeing Jack had his eyes closed already, she leant over to her bag and chose a new card that she had made the night before, this one of a heart.

She concentrated. Jack concentrated. Time stretched. Light that had travelled a billion years, found their window and fell on their expectant faces.

At last Jack opened his eyes and said tentatively, 'A cross?'

Mel shuddered. The card she first picked must still have been imprinted on her mind; un-erased by that other.

Jack asked again.

Me swallowed. 'Yes.'

'You're lying?'

'No,' said Mel. 'Is that what you see?'

'Yes. I see a cross and I see you.'

Mel rubbed her shoulders like she was cold.

'What don't you like about crosses?' he asked.

One of their bike rides had taken them to the cemetery, where they'd run around, tracing the often illegible epitaphs with their fingers, calling out to each other what they could decipher of the moss- and weather-eaten words: 'Here lies … beloved daughter … soul-mate and confidante …'

Wonderboy

Strangely moved, Mel had asked if it were right that whole lives should be abridged to a sentence. Her and Jack's would fill a paragraph, surely? 'An entire book!' he'd assured her.

She was still looking glum.

'Well?' he pestered her.

She pondered how best to answer before leaning forward. 'When you look at the books in the library, don't you see the trees that went into making them?'

Jack cocked his head. 'I don't understand?'

'This, here, *our* book. For something good …' she murmured brokenly, '… something good always dies.'

Jack nodded. 'I didn't see it that way. But I will now.' Mel smiled. 'And I'll also see you.'

Her smile fell away. Gulping, she got up and ran out. Jack sat up and grabbed the cards, not noticing the heart, and put them aside. He followed her down the rope ladder.

Stepping out from under the Cubby House in his slippers, Jack let his eyes adjust to the night. He stumbled forth, but what he thought was Mel was in fact the long white stem of a tree. He returned to the Cubby House, leaving the light on. When he woke in the morning, it had been switched off and Mel lay unstirring beside him.

Chapter 16

Jack's house was frenetic with activity. The barbecue was today, and Jean was in a flap getting Daniel, Simon and Jack to see to the last details. Daniel had already set up trestle tables on the turning circle, covered with butcher's paper. Jack had laid out green and white serviettes on them, as well as hung streamers between the trees and porch posts, from which Simon had tied the balloons he'd blown up. Jean had busied herself, cooking indoors.

There was still the pile of junk near the shed, much to Jean's chagrin, but Daniel hid much of it with carefully positioned wood partitions, and stacked-up bales of hay. Jack finished laying out the plastic plates and cutlery, supplemented with crockery from indoors. Jean placed covered meat trays on a special table reserved for food. And Simon enjoyed the more exciting job of building up the woodpile for a great big bonfire to end the night.

Daniel fired up the barbecue (a steel plate on besser bricks) and threw the first half-dozen snags on it.

Jean gave one last inspection of the results. Nodding with satisfaction, she poured Daniel and herself champagne in two fluted plastic glasses.

Jack eyed Jean balefully.

'All right,' she capitulated, 'you can ask Mel!'

Jack whooped. Jean seemed to have softened after hearing Juliet was going away.

'And Juliet?' He figured he'd push his chances.

Jean paused. 'And *Mrs* Jeffries, too, if it isn't beneath her.'

Daniel winced.

'Thanks, Mum.'

Jack scampered off towards the stile between the two properties, Simon watching enviously, worried he might never have a girlfriend himself. Daniel nodded at Jean with thanks. She snorted and turned away.

It was late afternoon and the barbecue was well in progress. With Jean being on the school council, several teachers were present: Higgins, Miss Jackson and Miss Ashton, the school librarian. The other guests included many of Jack's classmates and their parents. Of the kids, among them there was Glen, Noel, Emma, Kate, Fatty and Michael. A couple of Simon's classmates were also present: Troy and Adrian.

Most of the men were gathered by the smoking barbecue in their shorts or slacks, talking loudly and drinking from their beer cans, discarding the pull-rings in the fire, and taking it in turns to char the steaks, snags and chicken legs and wings, while their cigarettes helped fuel the cloud they were ensconced in. The women were more spread out, on the chairs, under the trees, or inside doing the washing up, drinking either the punch or Porphyry Pearl, topping up the coleslaw or tomato, onion and cucumber salads. The kids were glugging soft drinks and eating the adults' food, enlivened with more exciting fair like fairy bread.

Although politics was usually assiduously avoided by the adults, today it dominated, with rather heated argument. The opposition party had blocked supply of budget Bills in the Senate. Whitlam was being forced into calling an early election.

His unprecedented reign of instituting progressive policy seemed destined for an abrupt end.

Jack and Mel stood slightly apart from the gathering, the shared, and rather more prosaic, thought perplexing their minds: no music!

They made their way into the gathering, only to collide with Miss Jackson's stringy form. They ran the other way, this time pulling up in front of Jean. She had just come from the house with a steaming mug of hot chocolate.

'Jack! Go and give your teacher this.'

'Miss Jackson?'

Jean squinted. 'Yes, of course Miss Jackson.'

'No.'

Jean's open mouth started to take the shape of a word, but Daniel got in first. 'It's all right, Jean, I'll take it.'

Always making excuses for the kid! Jean eyed her husband piercingly.

'No, Daniel,' she said firmly. 'I told Jack to do it'.

Jean shoved the hot chocolate in Jack's hand, a splash falling on the soft part between thumb and forefinger and slightly scalding him.

Jack looked at the brown liquid sloshing in the mug.

'She's ... she's a dalek,' he muttered. 'A dalek!'

Jean shot a glance at the other guests. Emma's mum was closest, but she was fortunately preoccupied in filling up her plate with potato salad, and taking to Mrs Harrow.

Jean leant in close and spoke between gritted teeth. 'Jack, take it to her. Do you hear me?'

Mel tugged gently on Jack's shirt. Pouting, he followed her in the direction of Miss Jackson but halted after only a dozen steps.

'I won't, Mel. I just won't. Nothing will make me give it to her.'

Mel hawked her throat and spat in the mug.

'I'm doing it.'

Miss Jackson turned sharply then looked relieved to see Jack was merely handing over a drink. He and Mel removed themselves to one of the piles of hay bales that were hiding the junk, and took their watch.

Miss Jackson blew on the skin of the hot chocolate.

'Oh, look, a marshmallow,' she murmured to Miss Ashton.

Miss Jackson took a swig before hearing Jack and Mel guffaw. She watched them run away.

Not having any other classmates their age to play with, Simon, Troy and Adrian settled on lining up the little kids to play Red Rover.

'Pick me, Simon!' yelled Noel.

'No, pick me!' cried Glen.

Fatty was fuming. '*I* wanna be captain,' he wheezed.

Troy laughed. 'You always wanna be captain, Fatty.'

'Yeah,' said Adrian. '*I'm* captain.'

'Well, who's the other captain?'

Troy looked at Fatty like he was the dumbest kid in the world. 'Me and Simon. You know how it works. Right, line up, you lot.'

The kids formed a group. Fatty tried to make the point that if one side could have two captains, why not the other, suggesting he share captaincy with Adrian. He was drowned out by derisive laughter.

Simon made the first choice. 'Noel.'

'Cool,' said Noel, not believing his luck at being chosen first. Adrian pointed out Bill.

Whilst Troy and Adrian were picking teams, Simon turned to Jack, a surly smile on his lips.

'Wanna play, Jack?'

Jack examined the kids already chosen and those squirming on the spot wishing they'd at least be saved the indignity of being picked last. True to form, Mel had the same sly expression on her face. The two nodded at each other then shook their heads firmly in the negative at Simon.

Mel tapped Fatty on the shoulder. 'What's your name?'

'Fatty,' he said.

Mel gently shook her head. 'No. What does your mum call you?'

Fatty stared at her a moment before mumbling, 'Shane.'

Mel gave him a wink. 'Shane, Jack and I have better games. I'm picking you first to join in. But everyone can play.' She touched Jack. 'You're it.'

Shane bellowed at the top of his lungs, 'Chasey!'

Mel took Shane's hand, and they ran off together. Simon, Troy and Adrian watched as the other kids also forgot the game of Red Rover and followed after them. Jack touched Adrian on the hand.

'You're it!'

Adrian tried to swipe him back but Jack snaked out of the way.

'Uh, uh,' he said, wagging a finger. 'Count to twenty, remember.'

Jack fled in the direction of the barbecue, presently manned by Michael's dad. Simon petitioned Troy and Adrian to hold their ground, but Adrian quickly counted the last five seconds and touched Troy.

'You're it!' yelled Adrian, fleeing.

Simon grabbed Troy's arm before he, too, could abandon him. Troy looked down at his hand in Simon's before laughing and snatching it away.

'You like me too much,' he said almost inaudibly, and was gone.

Simon stood still a long moment, a tremble in his every joint, before distractedly helping himself to food he knew he would never be able to eat. Nothing was certain anymore for him except this fact: somehow Jack was to blame for usurping the usual rights of passage. Somehow Jack, three years his junior, was the first to get a girlfriend. That bloody girl!

Spitting out a slice of fairy bread, he passed by Miss Jackson and Miss Ashton. Miss Jackson was helping herself to the punch, with Miss Ashton whispering in her ear.

'Marcia, I'm sure Jean could make you another hot chocolate.'

'Hot chocolate! Lydia, am I a child?'

Miss Jackson sculled the punch, then wobbled, backing into the fold-out table on which the punch bowl rested, nearly sending both flying. Miss Ashton dragged her friend away, but not before Miss Jackson had filled another glass, managing to slop much of it on them both.

Bloody adults! Simon sat down on a hay bale, leaning back on a few more piled behind him, feeling their prickly texture and taking in their sunny smell. He leant back further and nearly got swallowed in a gap between two bales. Peering through, he could see Juliet standing alone, looking awkward, an undrunk glass of punch held delicately in her hands. Behind her, Jean was talking to Mrs Holroyd. Simon adjusted his position to spy Daniel approaching the two, holding a plate of crisps.

Jean, one of the few adults not discussing politics, was halfway through a comment to Mrs Holroyd but with her eyes on Juliet. 'See what I mean, Jane? How she dresses to the nines? Can't be all that hard being a single mother, after all.'

Daniel held up the plate of food. 'Care for something else to chew on?'

Jean started at the uncharacteristic sarcasm in her husband's voice. Jane Holroyd waved away the food, and Jean did likewise. Daniel's eyes sidled across to Juliet who was affecting profound fascination in the failed rose climber he'd made for Jean.

Mrs Holroyd leaned closer to Jean. 'And tell me about this girl of hers. My Glen says she's a real upstart, always talking in class.'

'Well,' said Jean, warming to the theme, 'she hasn't been good for Jack, I can tell you.'

From the corner of her eye, she spied Daniel putting down the plate of food and walking up to Juliet with a glass of punch of which he'd availed himself.

'His father's made him dreamy enough as it is ...' Jean mumbled.

Mrs Holroyd followed Jean's fixed gaze to see Daniel clinking his glass with Juliet's.

Daniel wished he were meeting Juliet at the stile bridging their properties, not here, not in front of all these small minds and prying eyes. Goodness knows he'd had scant amount of her company; he coveted every second for himself.

They mutely sipped their drinks.

'I'm sorry,' said Juliet, breaking the silence.

'I know,' said Daniel. 'Looks like the bastards are out to get him. Whitlam had made me proud to be Australian again.'

Juliet smiled. 'Yes, that too. But I specifically meant the way I spoke to you on the phone the other night.'

Daniel nodded. 'It's okay. It was all true.'

Juliet glanced down at her glass, neither knowing how to proceed from that remark.

'Juliet,' Daniel at last ventured, 'Jack says you're very ill.'

Simon, who was still sitting the other side of the hay bales, sat up straight and tuned in.

'If there's anything I can – '

Juliet cut Daniel off. 'No.' She softened her tone. 'It's terminal, Dan. I've been given three months.'

A part of Daniel caved in on itself, bringing down the rickety roof of his self-possession and exposing a soul until then mostly successfully inured to the elements.

Juliet merely smiled at his pallor and turned to behold the beautiful sunset now cupping the hills to the west.

Trusting his voice at last, Daniel asked, moved, 'Why come back here?'

Juliet remained focused on the hills, as if in their dwindling light was an answer to her own imminent dissolution. She finally faced Daniel, fixing his eyes.

'Because I couldn't get out of my head a boy I met as a girl in a magical garden.'

Daniel's heart stopped. Had she always felt the same way too, then?

Juliet sighed. 'But now I think that could never have happened.'

His heart beat again, faster to make up for the lost ones. Sweat pricked his brow.

'Mel?' he stuttered.

Simon's eyes screwed up tighter on hearing that girl's name. He swivelled round to peer through the narrow gap in the hay bales.

Juliet sipped the punch. Usually, she would have found its sweetness unpleasant but now its sugariness was a hit, a rush of life.

'Dash will look after her.'

Daniel understood finally. Dash was Mel's father. He blurted before he could stop himself, 'She's your love child!'

Juliet sipped the last of her punch. Daniel remembered his own glass and quickly drained it before taking hers and plonking both down on the hay bale. His glass rolled off the other side and hit Simon on the head. Simon caught it in his lap so it wouldn't smash on the ground and perhaps bring them to his side of the barricade.

Daniel reached for Juliet but, with an immense effort of will, stayed his hand. If Mel was Juliet and Dash's love child, what then of that comment about a boy in a magical garden, the very garden he had painted them in, which she couldn't get out of her mind?

She turned a flushed and tear-stained face to his, a secret raging under that eloquent and beauteous countenance.

'Oh Daniel, I wanted a kid with a wonderful man and it turned out they're hard to come by. I inquired after you but ...'

She glanced at Jean.

Daniel then knew the second secret just as instinctively. How had they lost that, their silent communion? When the two were kids, it was as though they could read each other's minds. A gift only now could they reclaim. Dash was not a rival. Not at all. Because ...

'He's gay,' whispered Daniel.

Simon's eyes opened wide.

Juliet shot Daniel a pained glance. With the pall of suspicion over Dash, she knew how some prejudiced minds conflated homosexuality with child abuse.

The news roiled Simon's stomach. For a brief second, he glimpsed a loathsome affinity between him and that teacher. He pushed it away, chiding himself for his weakness and instead forced glee to animate his features. Mr Rush gay – wait till he taunted Jack with that!

Juliet took Daniel's arms. He gripped hers in turn. Jean, who had been trying to focus on her conversation with Mrs Holroyd, could no longer pretend she wasn't distracted, and hurried towards them.

'Dan, about Dash and Jack,' murmured Juliet, 'do you believe this – '

'Daniel,' interrupted Jean coldly. 'I'm sure it's time you took another plate round to the guests.'

Daniel looked at his wife as if she were an alien. She recoiled from his profound scientific detachment. His eyes slipped off hers and onto the other gossipers watching them.

'You know, Juliet,' he said, still embracing her. 'You and Mel coming here ... well, it's been the best ... well, the best thing ...'

Juliet let go of his arms, but he still fervently gripped hers. She glanced round, painfully conscious of their audience. Daniel at last became aware of them too.

Something got lost in his voice.

'... for Jack, I mean,' he concluded quietly.

Letting go of Juliet, Daniel picked up a tray of lamingtons and stumbled off. Juliet stared at the inquisitive throng before making her way to the nearest children's voices. She would find Mel and leave. Or leave Mel if she wished to stay. But either way, she had to get out of there.

Simon climbed up the hay bales, then jumped down, landing beside Jean. He tugged on her arm excitedly.

'Hey, Mum! Where's Jack?'

Jean glared at him. 'How the hell should I know?'

She headed to the house after throwing a defiant glance at those still staring. Simon didn't think he could recall a time in recent memory when his mother had snapped at him like that. He balled his fist and set off in search of Jack.

He approached the shed that Daniel and Jack spent so much time in of late. His hunch was a good one, for Jack came running round the corner, colliding with him.

'Umph!' they cried.

Jack was the first on his feet. 'Are you it?' he asked.

Simon shook his head impatiently, standing also and dusting the dirt off his trousers. 'No.'

'Well, you are now!'

Jack hit Simon on the shoulder and tried to run off but Simon grabbed him by the waist.

Jack wrestled with him. 'Let go! Twenty seconds, remember!'

Simon pulled Jack in closer, digging his fingers into his brother's arm.

'Simon!'

'Shut up!'

Simon pushed his face into Jack's. 'You know who Mel's dad is? Mr Rush!'

Gauging Jack's expression, this was old news. Simon felt a surge of disappointment but quickly rallied. He'd see the effect of that other, better secret.

'Well, you won't know this: he's a *poof*!'

Jack tried to lean away from his brother's hot, acrid breath. 'What do you mean?'

'Mr Rush, that perv that touched you. Well, he's a poof!'

Jack struggled but his brother was too strong. Jack had heard that word before, used by the older kids at school – but he didn't yet know what it meant. He started to yell. Worried the noise might bring the adults, Simon shook him hard and pushed him against the side of the shed.

He twisted Jack's arms till they stung with pain. 'Say it, Jack: Mel's dad's a poof.'

Jack began to cry despite himself. The last person he ever wanted to cry in front of was his brother. He felt a hot shame turning his skin red.

'Say it, Jack, say it,' taunted Simon, desperate the words would act as an exorcism on himself.

Jack stopped crying suddenly and beheld his brother with absolute hatred. 'All right, Simon, Mel's dad's a poof. Mel's dad's a poof.'

They were just words: stupid, meaningless words.

Simon eased his grip, frightened by the state he'd got his brother in. He looked round; surely an adult would come any second. He no longer wanted to hear those words. Their incantation hadn't worked; Simon was still possessed.

Jean turned down the record player Daniel had brought out of the shed on Jack and Mel's insistence. Was that a kid yelling, was that …?

Jack had Simon's arms now, holding him in a heated embrace. 'Mel's dad's a poof!' he spat in Simon's face.

'Jack, shut up! You'll get us in trouble.'

Jack threw Simon against the shed, surprised he was the one now doing the overpowering.

'Mel's dad's a poof!' he continued to shout. 'Mel's dad's a poof! Mel's dad's a …'

Jack's mouth shut in an instant for there, standing behind Simon, was Mel, staring at him with hurt and base betrayal writ large across her vulnerable face.

She burst into tears and ran, nearly knocking into Jean and Daniel. All the anger drained out of Jack, replaced with regret.

He pushed Simon to the ground, and chased after her. With a sickening drowning of his soul, he now understood what that word meant.

'No, Mel, wait!'

Simon got up, beholding his father and mother. He was about to say, 'See how he pushed me!' when their expressions silenced him, for it wasn't just his father that stared at him with horror, but uncharacteristically, his mother, too.

Her face matched his for guilt.

Jean quickly trawled back through events. Had Mel heard something of the words she had been saying to Mrs Holroyd, the way the two had been rubbishing mother and daughter alike? Why had she ever said Jack was a sissy? What if he was? Or what if … Simon!

Jean stared at Simon with new knowledge. That was why she had been so brutally supportive of his every sporting and physical endeavour – she'd nursed an unconscious terror for him.

Mel could hear Jack gaining on her. She ducked behind the hay bales, and weaved between unsightly tractor engines, rusted scarifiers and other farm detritus. She noted an old fridge lying on its back in the long grass that had grown up around it.

'Mel? Mel?'

She opened it up and jumped inside. The lid fell shut.

Chapter 17

Jean was standing talking quietly with Higgins, Miss Jackson and Miss Ashton. The sun had set and only the raging bonfire and porchlights lit their faces. Mrs Holroyd returned with the kids, whom she had gathered together and instructed to call Mel's name.

Mrs Holroyd switched off her flashlight and shook her head.

Miss Jackson turned her gaze from the search party to Jean.

'Look, I'm sure the little miss is just hiding,' she blurted, slurring her words. 'She's probably trying to teach the boys a lesson.'

Jean and Higgins shifted uncomfortably. They were relieved to see Daniel approaching with Jack.

'Any luck?' asked Jean.

'No. Juliet's going to keep searching at their place.'

Daniel turned to Mrs Holroyd. 'So you didn't have any luck either, I take it?'

Mrs Holroyd tried to smile. 'Look, I'm sure the little girl is just hiding.'

Jean and Higgins shared a glance: Mrs Holroyd's words had almost been an echo of Miss Jackson's, but without the lofty tone.

Mrs Holroyd turned to Jean. 'I'm sorry, Jean, we've got to get the kids home.'

Jean nodded.

'Glen! Sean!' yelled Mrs Holroyd. 'Get in the car!'

Michael, with his father and mother, Mr and Mrs Gimbol, walked up to the group. Mr Gimbol leant in to Daniel.

'Sorry, Dan, but the babysitter needs rescuing from this tyrant's younger brother.' Mr Gimbol ruffled his son's hair. 'They can both be – '

They looked up at the sound of a glass breaking. Miss Jackson had dropped her punch.

Wobbling, she addressed Jean. 'Yes, I'm sorry, Mrs. Bennett, but we ...' she indicated Miss Ashton, '... must say our goodbyes as well. I wouldn't worry too much. Children are always deceiving their parents. In my experience, they're all liars, every last one of them.'

The adults shifted uncomfortably. Higgins put a warning hand on Miss Jackson's forearm.

'Miss Jackson!'

She threw him off. 'Let me finish, Mr Higgins. You know, I wouldn't be surprised if that Mr Rush had something to do with this. The pervert!'

Jack, who had turned away by this time, stopped dead in his tracks and whirled around.

Higgins tried again to escort her away. 'Miss Jackson. Marcia ... please!'

He tried to take her elbow but she shook him off.

'In my opinion, he's still here, preying on kids.'

Jean felt herself near panic. 'Marcia, enough!' she balled, fearful. Fearful of what all their rumour-mongering had done.

For where on earth was Mel?

Jack was starting to comprehend exactly what had happened to Dash. He looked first at Higgins and then Miss Jackson with hatred, but especially at the latter. Then, with equally unsympathetic eyes, his gaze fell on the general circle.

Miss Jackson would not be silenced. 'I don't know why you're shushing me, Jean. He touched your – '

'He didn't touch me.'

Everyone in the throng went quiet and turned to Jack. Miss Jackson was the first to regain composure.

'What would you know? Frank, you saw that Mr Rush touching Jack.'

All eyes turned on Higgins.

'Well, yes … no. I mean, I did see him put a hand on Jack's shoulder.'

Daniel looked down at his hand on Jack's shoulder. Leaving it there, he addressed Higgins with disbelief.

'Is that *all*?

Higgins rubbed his hands guiltily. 'Well, I …'

Miss Jackson could see every adult in the group hanging their heads, bar Daniel, for the way they had contributed to the gossip. She saw she was losing the argument and shook Miss Ashton.

'Miss Ashton heard what he said in the library!' she screamed hysterically.

All eyes were now upon Miss Ashton. She spoke in a meek, faltering voice.

'Well, I suppose you could say he was just responding to the picture Jack drew, calling a spade … a spade.'

Miss Jackson went red. 'Yes, but what about all that stuff about Greeks performing in the nude?'

There was no answer to this until Jean stepped forward, her head bowed. 'Well, um, apparently Mel asked about that. I guess kids are … curious.'

Daniel looked at Jean sadly.

Miss Jackson faltered for a few seconds before getting back her wind.

'Then it's that girl causing all the trouble. Just look at what she's doing now, hiding to get attention!'

Jack's eyes drilled into Miss Jackson.

'I know the type. They're low-down, filthy scum. But worst of all ... far, far worse ... they're liars. All of them. Liars, liars, liars ...'

Jack's jaw set in anger, as Miss Jackson continued to rant. Recent episodes flashed through Jack's head. Miss Jackson telling Michael: 'Don't lie, I saw you.' Higgins saying to Jack: 'Don't lie, Jack.' Mel saying to Jack after she'd sent a card in the Cubby House: 'You're lying.' Mel saying to Jack: 'I would never lie to you, Jack. Never.'

He shook his head free of the broiling torrent of memories.

They had taken away Dash, which meant Juliet was going too, and that of course meant Mel. These lies had cost him his best friend.

He threw himself at Miss Jackson, his arms flailing into her.

'Liar! Liar! Liar!' he yelled at the top of his lungs.

For a moment, everyone watched, too startled to react, as Miss Jackson, overwhelmed, began screaming. The noise attracted the other kids to gather around with their parents. Something in Miss Jackson's cries made Jack pause. There was a wounded, frightened girl behind those accusing eyes. Mel's words came to him; her plea to remember Miss Jackson was lost but that they weren't. He withdrew his attack, but he could not yet forgive. He understood, somehow, that his greatest scorn should be reserved for Higgins.

Daniel, the first to get his wits about him, stepped forward and held Jack. 'Jack … Hush, son.'

Jean knelt beside him. 'Why did you hit her?'

Her old tone was gone; she genuinely wished to hear.

Daniel had to struggle to keep Jack still.

He looked his mum in the face. '*She* hit *me*.'

Jack lifted the hair off his split ear. Jean winced and touched it tenderly before turning to Miss Jackson. Michael stepped forward to stand alongside Jack.

'And me. She hit me too.'

All eyes refocused on Miss Jackson. The accusation was obviously news to Michael's parents; they clasped their arms around their son protectively. Miss Jackson, even in her drunken state, realised she had gone too far, and started backing away.

'Oh, I see. You're going to listen to the word of two filthy brats over an adult. Is that right?'

She turned to Higgins for one last vain petition of support. 'Mr Higgins?'

Higgins looked down, no longer willing to bail her out of trouble.

'*Et tu*? Well ... well! Miss Ashton, take me home, please.'

Miss Ashton seemed unable to move.

'Now!'

Reluctantly, Miss Ashton took pity on her friend and escorted her to their car, Miss Jackson throwing one more defiant look at the others.

'Well, where the hell were the listeners when *I* was a child?'

Jean glanced at Higgins interrogatively. Higgins could barely meet her gaze. Her focus shifting, Jean caught Simon's eye. Her elder son looked away, ashamed. Jean swallowed dryly; she knew she was guilty herself. Daniel continued to stroke Jack's hair. The anger had abated in Jack, leaving him in shock. Daniel eyeballed Higgins.

'I think you'd best go home as well. All of you.'

In a moment of crystal clear clarity, Jean beheld her husband. He alone in the town, had never engaged in idle gossip, had never run another person down, had always found the best in people, the things to praise. Mount Miller was a place where everyone knew everyone else's business, and what they didn't know, they made up. Daniel alone was exempt.

She watched him with these people, and the whole scene flipped for her. These people she saw as superior to him, superior in their tastes, their interests, ambitions, were all the fainter to her now, the less real, the apparitions. What were they next to this tower of a man? And yet *she* had looked down on *him*!

With a shock that made her tremble, she realised for the first time in their long marriage that she loved her husband. Then, with a second shockwave of heartbreaking, ecstatic emotion, she saw that meant she finally loved Jack also, for he was his father's son. Overwhelmed with motherly relief, she kneeled and pulled him to her breast, kissing his confused, crying eyes for forgiveness.

God, what had happened to Mel and what part had she played in her running off?

The last car drove away. Jean rose and regarded Daniel. She understood she had never really claimed her husband's heart and there was only one chance left to her.

To give him up completely now.

'Go to Juliet, Dan.'

Dan looked at her, pain in his eyes.

'She must be beside herself. Take Jack. Go to her. Go!'

Daniel nodded. He took Jack's hand. Jean went over to Simon standing dazed, and rested her hands on his shoulders. 'What have we done, Simon? What have … *I* done?'

She swivelled Simon round to face her and kneeled down. 'Simon, I want you to know something. I don't care who you end up loving.'

'Mum …'

'And if I ever meet anyone who does mind, I'll tear their throats out.'

Taking a torch, Daniel walked with Jack towards the fence dividing his property from Juliet's. Why had he stayed in this town? He'd seen it for what it was as a kid. It beat down the people who dared dream the world better. He spied Juliet coming the other way, without a torch. Maybe her eyes were adjusted to the dark. He turned off his torch but knew from her expression, and the fact she was alone, that she had failed to find Mel.

'Jack, have you any idea where Mel might have gone?' he asked his son. 'Some secret place you had?'

'The Cubby House?' Jack ventured, realising he'd never actually climbed up the manhole that led to the roof and the view over his house. Perhaps he hadn't wanted to twin the two worlds.

'I can look again but …' said Juliet, hopelessly.

Daniel stood up in a passion, grabbing Jack by the shoulders. 'Juliet, we'll find her. And when we do … well, you and Mr Rush, you've got to take Jack with you.'

He thrust Jack forward who stumbled and turned round.

'Dad!' he cried.

Juliet looked from Jack to Daniel. 'Then you don't believe Dash is ...'

Daniel took her hands. 'No. What I do believe is this is a small, narrow-minded town, and it will kill any spirit of difference in anyone who remains in it. And I know this most of all: you've got to take Jack.'

He thrust Jack at Juliet again.

'Dad!' screamed Jack.

Juliet, crying, patted down Jack's hair and tried to push him back.

'Dan ...' she moaned.

Daniel was still wild in his eyes. 'Please take him.' He began almost talking to himself. 'I'll talk Jean into it somehow.' He lunged forward and took her arms, which were caressing Jack protectively. 'But, Juliet, we can't have this happen twice.'

Juliet stifled a sob. Jack, crushed between them, looked up, scared.

'Have what happen twice?' he yelled.

Daniel remained gazing at Juliet. 'Losing our garden.' He clutched her fervently. 'It was real, Juliet. We made it real for a moment. I remember it too.'

Juliet stared at him. Her expression of longing was mixed with horror. 'But you forget ...' She slapped her right temple. 'It's in my head, Dan. My mind, it's eating my mind!'

Daniel clutched her head and kissed it. 'I'll burn it out with my thoughts. I'll ...'

Jack stared at his father at these words.

'We *could* once do that, couldn't we?' murmured Juliet. 'We could sense each other from miles away … We've got it back!' She blinked. 'But we couldn't sense when my mum was killed in that crash or your dad after he hung himself, could we? This was it, this life.'

Daniel and Juliet looked into each other's eyes with the same sudden thought. Juliet's face went ashen.

'No, no, Juliet, I'm sure – ' Dan tried to comfort.

'No, Dan. Mel … we can't sense her.'

Juliet turned and hurried back through the ghost gums, disappearing amid the inky blackness like an apparition. Daniel fell on the ground, his head bent over, moaning. Jack fled to a tree and hid behind it.

A terrible premonition came over Daniel that he would never see Juliet again. He looked up, trying to get one more glance. But she had slipped from his world for a second and final time.

Jack ventured from his hiding place behind the tree. His father was an artist too – his father and Juliet had also read each other's minds. Then … how did it go wrong? He reached out and touched his father on the shoulder.

'Dad … why did you give up?'

Daniel shot a surprised and pained glance at Jack. 'What, son?'

'Mr Higgins said you used to paint pictures.'

Daniel sighed, and wearily got to his feet. 'Well, I had you and your brother and your mum to support.' He turned away, dangerously near tears, his greatest fear. 'But don't *you* give up, Jack. You're a better artist at eleven than I am at thirty-six. And far more courageous. Don't ever give up, do you hear!'

Daniel scanned the trees desperately. Jack gently took his hand. This seemed to reignite the wildness in Daniel and he knelt down again, grabbing Jack by the shoulders.

'Dad! You're hurting me!'

'Whatever happens, Jack, I'm going to give you the life I should have had. You won't fight anyone's wars but your own, you'll never take another's life and live with the nightmare of that, you'll …'

Jack pulled away from his father, and ran back to the house. For the first time, in search of his mum.

Chapter 18

His bedroom door slightly ajar, Jack peered through the gap into the living room. Jean and Daniel were speaking to two policemen: Constable Rafter and Lieutenant Speers.

Rafter was the older with short black hair, a square face, once harsh but now relaxed and worn. Speers was young and gangly with a face that looked like it had been in a press; all nose.

'Mr and Mrs Bennett,' Rafter was saying, his police cap held in his hands, 'like I told Mrs Jeffries, I'm sure she'll turn up soon enough. Kids do this sort of thing all the time. It's just their way of getting attention.'

Jean could barely control her anger. 'An eleven-year-old girl goes missing, and you think it's an attention-grabbing exercise?'

Speers spoke in a nasally, slightly snotty voice. 'Calm down, Mrs ...'

Daniel cut him off. 'Look, officer, don't tell my wife to calm down.'

Speers seemed on the point of retorting but Rafter waved him down.

'Take your hat off inside, son.'

Annoyed, Speers took off his hat. The two silently conversed, wondering how they could defuse the situation. Jean and Daniel surveyed each other also. They realised it was the first time they had shown support for each other.

Jack bumped the door with his leg, the soft noise causing Daniel to turn and spot him through the crack. Jean, Rafter and

Speers followed his gaze. Daniel gestured that they should move away.

Jack closed the door. He crawled onto his bed, grabbing the telepathy cards in the process. He held his temples and tried sending a message.

'Mel? Mel? Are you reading me, over? Mel?

Frustrated, he pushed the cards off his bed. They fanned out on the floor. He was just about to turn out the light when he noticed the new heart card. He picked it up with infinite care.

'Mel …?'

Sitting down on his bed again, he tried sending the heart instead. Tried with all his might. Giving up, finally, he turned out his light, and pulled the cover over his head. What had Daniel and Juliet said? They could sense the living. They could sense those with life in them. But once they passed out of this world, they sensed them no more. For this was it. This life was all there was.

If this life was all there was, and dream, and the aspiring imagination counted for nothing, then Jack knew he had best be done with it now.

The old fridge glowed in the moonlight.

A sliver of light passed over his eyes.

A sigh moved the grass outside his window.

All was quiet.

Jack's eyes snapped open and he sat up in bed as Mel entered through the wall as a mist, before becoming whole and substantial. She was in a white, gossamer dress, like the one she'd greeted him in during their shared fantasy of the secret garden.

She was humming the plaintive chords of *Polovtsian Dances*.

'Mel,' he whispered. 'I'm ... I'm sorr...'

Mel smiled warmly and leant over him. 'Shhh.' She tapped him on the shoulder. 'You're it!'

She half stepped back through the wall, as if falling into a lake.

'No, Mel,' pleaded Jack, grabbing her hands.

She winked. 'I'll show you.'

Jack let go and stepped back. 'I can't.'

Now only her head was still visible, sinking back through the wall. 'Yes, you can. We're going to play the game of Hide and Seek.'

Her head bobbing under the surface, Jack found his courage and tried to step after her but instead crashed into the plaster. Coming to his senses, he ran to the next room.

Mel was walking through the front windows, the curtains either side slightly moving.

She turned her head back to him, her chin resting on her shoulder. 'Don't give up, Jack. You always give up.'

The night enveloped her outside. Jack stood there a moment, looking at the panes with their slight breath of condensation. His eyes then wandered to the door handle. His expression changed to one of joy. He'd catch her all right!

He checked behind the Cunningham Casuarina, where the moon perched in its topmost branches. She wasn't there.

Spinning round slowly, he just had time to glimpse her stepping round the corner of the house, doing her own pirouette in turn.

'Don't give up, Jack.'

Jack sprinted after her.

He came to a halt at the wall of hay bales. Breaching them at their weakest point, he made his way amongst the junk Daniel had tried to hide.

'Don't give up now,' came Mel's voice, mellifluous and clear.

He spotted the old fridge and walked up to it. Kneeling down, he leant on it a moment as though it were a coffin, laying his split ear on its cold surface and listening for a heartbeat. Sitting up, he pulled at the handle, throwing it open with one sudden flourish.

His voice was triumphant.

'I've found you!

Chapter 19

Jack pedalled to the gate. Simon was behind him, for once not trying to overtake. Jack stopped to look at the 'For Sale' sign on the next-door neighbour's fence.

Simon swung their own gate open, waiting for Jack to pass through, before shutting it and pedalling alongside him.

'Come on, Jack. I'll ride with you.'

Simon matched Jack's slow speed as they weaved their way through the up-and-down hills, the shadows shortening across the land to a wan thought.

When they got to the outskirts of town, Jack found himself staring at the houses gliding past, with their ubiquitous looped wire fences, all painted white. With their nearly identical letter boxes, sagging verandas, and neat gardens of flowers and fruit trees, they merged into a single shot, the postcard of the generic country town dwelling.

He found himself humming the Kinks' 'Dead End Street'. Soon he was imaging the inhabitants of the houses stepping out in their Sunday best to wave at him as he passed, then already standing at their letter boxes, and lastly stepping from their gates and joining together in a conga line, that followed as a train endlessly coupled, endlessly shunted alongside him. The baker, the fireman, the grocer, the butcher, Mr Sloane who owned the record store where he'd bought Grieg's *Morning Mood*, all dancing, all chanting,

Dead end street, dead end street

What had he been imagining on that morning he first saw Mel?

That's right, that a Cessna dusting crops was become a World War II spitfire. He'd thrown himself in the siding, now a trench in his mind, and fired off a full magazine in the air, the stick in his hand transformed to a Sten gun.

How his imaginings had changed since then, losing their militaristic edge, to become more sophisticated, more intricately devised and sensitive.

He pedalled harder, Simon matching him, to catch up to the front of the conga line, being led by Dash, of course, a Pied Piper clapping hands in time to the music, Mel skipping beside him.

'Dead end street,' they whispered, 'Dead end street.'

'Head to the feet,' he mumbled, noting Simon glancing at him. They turned up the road that led to their school.

It was clear to Jack there was another consequence of a wholesale surrender to wonder … The more it became obvious that there was a massive, seemingly unbridgeable gap between imagination and reality, the greater the temptation to flee, to form sides as it were, with one or the other. Reality, and become like Higgins or Miss Jackson. Straddle the two, and be like his father, lost to both. Accept dream altogether and …

The consequence of that last option opened up like a fissure in his mind to swallow him whole. He mentally retreated from its edge and shook himself as he and Simon came to a stop at the school gate.

So many gates.

'See you at lunch?' asked Simon.

Jack stared blankly. Simon had never asked that before.

'Red Rover,' explained Simon, lightly punching Jack in the shoulder. 'You're on my team.'

'Chasey,' said Jack.

'Eh?'

Jack stared at him.

'Okay, sure.'

'Give everyone a chance to work in the vineyard,' he said.

'Vineyard?' Simon looked at his brother guiltily. This was beyond him. He groped for a response. 'Chasey, definitely.'

Jack smiled faintly. Simon walked through the gate, glancing back nervously a few times. Jack looked around. First, at the monkey bars, and heard his own voice from the past floating forward to catch up with him.

'Come on, Noel, you've gotta cross.'

'Nah,' replied Noel, 'I'm playing Red Rover.'

How Jack had ached for a friend who liked his sort of games.

His eyes wandered to the empty oval. It erupted with the disembodied voices of a dozen kids aching to be chosen.

'Pick me.'

'No, pick me.'

'No, me.'

Those that worked longer in the garden ...

Next, Troy's voice, rising above the pleas, 'Who do ya reckon, Simon?'

... receive the same reward.

Simon, at last replying, 'Jack.'

Jack's eyes next strolled to the steps leading into his classroom.

'Jack!' came Miss Jackson's voice down from the past.

'Yes, Miss Jackson?' he'd returned.

'Jack, I didn't say you could get up. Sit down. Sit down at once! Jack!'

'Jack?'

It was Simon calling him now, in the present. He must have returned. Jack shook himself of his memories, and looked at his brother standing on the other side of the gate. In his head, Jack could still faintly hear the conga line singing 'Dead End Street'. He wanted to join it.

'Jack … please.'

To Jack's astonishment, Simon was near tears.

'From now on, you can rely on me,' Simon said, mastering his emotion. He then forced a laugh. 'Hey, who knows? I might even be calling on my younger brother for help some day too.'

It was with all his reserves of strength and will, that Jack at last he stepped through the gate.

Constable Rafter was leaning against the squad car while Lieutenant Speers' fingers toyed edgily with the strap on his gun holster. Before them, Daniel was standing only in boxers, axe in hand, staring down with venom at the fridge. Jean was on her knees in her nightie, arms wrapped round the pole of the turned veranda post, issuing a pitiful wail.

From the house, the radio was blaring the breaking news: the Governor-General had sacked the Whitlam government. People were protesting in the streets and it looked like wide-scale rioting might start.

With a sudden fury, Daniel let fly at the fridge, bringing the axe down hard upon it.

Speers stepped forward, reaching for his gun, but Rafter was ready and yanked it away. He pulled the young cop close and shook his head. The rookie had a lot more to see of life to know sadness, rage and disappointment was normal. Daniel had always seemed to Rafter one of the sanest in town, but that just made it all the more his turn to crack.

Daniel swung the axe down upon the fridge, blow after blow, the tin denting, the paint flying away in peels, the blade sparking, while Jean cried repeatedly for him to stop. Soon her shouts were replaced by sobs.

At last the blade broke off, and then the handle split when he kept going. When that broke in two, he fell on his knees before the fridge and beat it with his hands. When his strength waned, he merely slapped it.

Jean, whose arm was raised towards him, stood and staggered forth from the veranda. Her hands found his shoulders, and then she half collapsed on him, wrapping her arms around his so he could no longer bruise and bloody them.

They found her instead, and the two embraced.

Rafter felt his throat tightening. He tapped Speers on the shoulder and indicated the car.

They drove away with Daniel and Jean sobbing together in the dust, and Whitlam ceding defeat over the radio, as he counselled the faithful to 'Maintain your rage and enthusiasm …'

Miss Jackson was packing up her things. Higgins watched as she took the last item from her desk drawer, a silver hip flask and turned, noticing him for the first time.

Her features were drawn, pained, but her eyes were steely. Higgins leant against the wall, swallowed and then began what he should have said forty years earlier.

'Marcia, I knew. I knew our teacher, Mr Cord, was abusing you. All of us kids knew. I said nothing. As a penance, I've been so vigilant ever since. So vigilant I ... I went after the wrong target. A good man. A far more gifted teacher than I ... And helped destroy a family. For that I'm immeasurably sorry and, for failing you, I'm sorry to the very core of my being.'

He had found his eyes downcast but now looked up pleadingly.

'Forgive me.'

Miss Jackson walked straight past him, shoving the whiskey flask in his hands.

As he heard her steps echo down the corridor, he worried he might quiver to the floor where he would be found by the students. Only the sound of the morning bell gave him strength enough to push himself away from the wall.

A hundred kids could be heard clattering into class.

Chapter 20

Jack was sitting at the back of class, alone. Around him, the other kids were whispering. Michael had been going to occupy the seat beside him, but felt it would be disrespectful. Too soon. Higgins, who had escaped to the bathroom, re-entered. His guilty eyes betrayed him by seeking out Jack's.

Higgins lay his books down on the teacher's desk then found his voice.

'Okay, I'm taking this class for the rest of the year. Get out your books.'

He turned to write on the blackboard, glad he did not have to face the children, many of whom had been at that ... barbecue.

The students all took up their pens, except Jack who stared straight ahead, unmoving. In his head, he was playing the Kinks song that he had decided most encapsulated him.

'Wonderboy' summed up for Jack in the profoundest way everything that was wrong, but also right, with life. Here were the Kinks singing about how things could be whatever you wanted them to be through the sheer power of imagination, the unfettered will to make-believe, by refusing to accept that this is all there is. And running alongside this optimism a wistful refrain that surfaced in the song like a cold splash in the face: a reminder of the seemingly irreconcilable conjunction of dream and reality.

Life is only ...
Life is only ...

He and Mel were ready to re-imagine this wondrous and troubling world together, this world that's somehow only half thought through, and yet now here he was, left to his single mind's conjurings, alone and deeply lonely.

A Wonderboy without his muse.

He found himself in a sun-drenched cornfield with Dash and Mel, singing to the song, singing, singing.

> *Wonderboy, life's just begun,*
> *Turn your sorrow into wonder*

Next, they were in a crowded street, where grey faces searched for light amid corridors of dullness. Mel pulled Jack in close and sang:

> *Everybody's looking for the sun*
> *People strain their eyes to see*
> *But I see you and you see me*
> *And ain't that wonder?*

But she and Dash were fading away, and that refrain, that trembling, insistent, lingering question returned:

> *Life is only ...*

'Jack.'

> *Life is only ...*

'Jack?'

Life is lonely.

'Jack!'

Higgins was waving his hand in front of Jack's eyes, panic on his face. Jack seemed not to see it, then, as Higgins lowered his hand, he looked up boldly at the headmaster. Higgins' eyes lowered, and spied Jack's drawing. His face filled with admiration. The drawing depicted Jack's fantasy walk with Rush and Mel, the only colour among great, towering blocks of grey.

Higgins, emotional, put a hand on Jack's shoulder. Jack snarled and pulled his shoulder away. Higgins broke down and placed his hand on the desk.

'Forgive me ... please.'

Higgins began crying, great big heaving tears.

Jack felt himself sliding towards the precipice of insanity, of illogical, maddening dream.

'Don't give up, Jack,' echoed Mel's voice. He teetered on the cliff's edge.

'Don't ever give up.'

Jack turned from the dream in his head that he'd now got out on paper. If he could never wholly retreat into music and imagination, what would be his 'other' way? A wholesale death by reality? Or ... or perhaps a transmutation of one to the other? A saving grace in alchemy?

What Jack felt most in this music he'd come to love – the Kinks, Borodin, Delibes, Grieg, Tchaikovsky – this soaring, aching, maudlin, passionate, sad music – was that people had felt and been hurt deeply. It made him feel less alone but also fearful of what was to come.

He understood the solace his father found in music, the retreat and expression Juliet found in it, that Mel had shared, and realised it would become as valued, as necessary, as sustaining for him as for them. Indeed, that it already had acquired this significance, sustenance, support. In a way, a friend. A companion he could rely on for life, to connect with people living, but also people long dead through emotions as old as the hills but also as fresh, as raw, as each generation saw and experienced them.

In art, there is a truth failed at by life. Art is us at our best, our most communicative, honest, sensitive. As shocking and confronting as we have made nakedness, but every bit as natural and truthful, to the very core.

Dash had taught Jack to travel in time, and while his life might not always be wonderful, there were other lives he could dip into, be they in music, books or art. But he knew in one way, he would excel Dash, his father, and perhaps even Juliet, for he would also travel *forward* in time.

Because he would contribute to this greater life, because his art would one day comfort someone long after he was dead, would let that person know that someone else had seen the world as they do, has felt it as present, as alien, as beautiful, as confusing, and as tenuous in the grasp. But in the living, the striving to attain this higher life, lay the meaning, the merit.

He would tell his and Mel's story, not just in pictures, but also in words, and Mel needn't worry: it would fill a book.

Despite his heartbreaking sadness, he knew through Mel he'd tasted the best of life and, no matter what, he would never give up.

Jack reached forward. Higgins felt himself rising from a near drowning. He stopped sobbing and opened his eyes. The boy had taken his hand. That this boy should forgive him … this boy who should have nothing but rightful contempt for him … it was enough to go on with. He climbed out of the hole he'd dug in his own soul, and looked at Jack's drawing for a long time.

'It's brilliant, Jack.' He tousled the boy's hair. '*You* don't give up. You never will.'

Jack nodded with conviction. Higgins pulled himself together and walked to the blackboard. Jack looked down at his picture of Mel and smiled.

Thank you for the days…

THE END.

www.ingramcontent.com/pod-product-compliance
Lightning Source LLC
Chambersburg PA
CBHW031332170626
46807CB00002B/661